SOUL READER SERIES

BOOK 1: TOUCH ENABLED

DANTE F. LUPINETTI

ISBN-13: 978-1-7360396-1-8 (Paperback)
ISBN-13: 978-1-7360396-0-1 (eBook)

Bonus Content

How would you like to be a character in my next book in the Soul Reader Series? I will randomly select one of my fans who sign up for my newsletter.

Click https://www.subscribepage.com/soulreadersignup for a chance to be a character in my next book and to get exclusive access to the Soul Reader newsletter.

Table of Contents

1

The Hot DC News Market

When the cherry blossoms of spring gave way to the sweltering heat of summer, the nation's capital transformed from a winsome southern plantation into the nation's armpit. The manicured lawns and stately white buildings visited by adoring crowds seemed less attractive when shrouded in humidity.

As Zeke Jackson packed for his long trip from Lincoln, Nebraska, to Washington, DC, to start a new job at WJOP, his father looked at the showcase he had built to house his son's awards and trophies for news reporting. He pulled out the statue of a reporter with his sleeves rolled up, pen in hand, writing on a tablet.

"Ah," said Zeke, "KOLN's On the Beat Award. My first in 2016."

Zeke's dad put it back and pulled out another. Zeke's eyes teared up. The Lincoln Community Award, 2018. Zeke won it for his coverage of a local church's outreach to the homeless.

"Should I continue?" asked Zeke's dad.

"No…no…," said Zeke. "I…I…don't want to reminisce right now. I'll nev…never be able to leave."

"That's the idea, son. Your mother and I don't want you to go. You have everything you need right here in Lincoln: a family that loves you, a good job where you're doing great without a lot of stress, a community that loves you, a fifteen-minute commute to work. What more could you ask for?"

"A chal…chal…challenge," said Zeke. "I need a challenge. Washington, DC, is one of the top news markets in the country. No…no…self-respecting reporter would pass up a chance to work for the top news station in one of the top markets like DC." WJOP's news director Harvey Schmidt, a hard-shelled man with a soft center, had seen potential in Zeke and hired him to shore up his news department.

When Zeke finished packing, he put his luggage in his red Toyota pickup and came back inside the house to say his goodbyes. First, he embraced his mom, squeezing her tight. "I la…la…love you, Mom. I'll be home for Christmas."

"You better be," she said as she handed him a tin of cookies for the long ride.

Then he embraced his dad. "I la…la…love you, too, Pops," said Zeke.

"Well, if I can't change your mind, I might as well cheer you on," said his dad. "Godspeed, son."

"Oo...oops, I almost forgot. Where's Cucho?" asked Zeke. His dad yelled the dog's name, and Cucho came running. Zeke went down on one knee, and the big golden Lab jumped into his arms. Zeke wrapped his arms around the big dog as Cucho licked his face.

"I think he's gonna miss the dog more than us," said his mom.

"I think you're right, Joan," replied his father, Rodger.

"I'll call you when I get there," Zeke called out as he waved goodbye.

And with that Zeke walked out to his truck for the thousand-mile drive to Silver Spring, Maryland. He drove for ten hours before stopping at a Holiday Inn for the night. He got a sub from the Subway next door. That tided him over until the next morning.

He arose at 6:00 am, ate the free breakfast, and got back on the road. He arrived at the house he rented in Silver Spring at 1:00 pm.

The next morning, he reported for work.

Zeke stepped quickly along the sticky August sidewalk and up the long set of white stone steps toward the arched entrance of the white stone building. He clenched his right fist and punched the air. With a solid sense of confirmation, he shouted, "Yes!"

Zeke entered the building and stepped up to the receptionist. "I…I…I'm Zeke Ja—"

The pert redhead glanced up with a smile and interrupted him. "Harvey's expecting you," she said. "I'll show you to his office."

Zeke nodded. He cringed that his first words at his new job had already branded him. But he reminded himself that his reporting at CBS affiliate KOLN had won him several awards for investigative reporting and community affairs. Maybe he'd just been the reporter behind the anchor. They kept him off the air most of the time, but everyone knew the talking heads were reading Zeke's copy. People trusted Zeke. They believed what he wrote, and he'd built quite a following over the years.

"I'm Julie, Julie Stokes," she spoke over her shoulder as she led the way. "Harvey hired me a couple of years ago. He's a good boss. No nonsense, though." They climbed a flight of stairs. Zeke noticed her long shapely legs and the graceful way she navigated the steps in heels. They walked down a long well-lit corridor. Upon the walls hung plaques attesting to the solid reputation the station had earned over the years. One plaque in particular caught Zeke's eye. Embossed with an image of the Pentagon and the World War II statue of marines raising the flag, it read:

> The Pentagon recognizes WJOP's accurate, heroic 9/11 coverage in the face of harm's way.

Zeke stopped to read another plaque, but Julie motioned with her right hand and said, "Come on. You can read those later."

When they arrived at the news director's office at the end of the corridor, Julie entered without hesitation. "Good morning, Harvey. Here's your new hire." Looking at Zeke, she said, "Let me know if you need anything. Welcome aboard the top news station in DC."

"Well, like the lady said, welcome to the top news station in DC," Harvey said. "And I mean to keep it that way." He reached into the top drawer of his desk, pulled out a cigar, and proceeded to light it without any concern. Smoke billowed above his desk and slowly drifted into the bullpen outside his office. "You don't smoke, do you, kid?"

"No…no, sir," said Zeke.

"Good. It's a nasty habit. The management tolerates my occasional indulgence, and nobody dares complain. Zeke, news has gone soft in the DC area. People are starting to mock the whole industry. We built our rep on truth-telling and integrity. I'm not going to listen to someone call us fake news after I spent twenty years building this department. I think you can help us, here."

"Ye…ye…ye…yes, sir," Zeke replied.

Harvey squinted at his new hire, shuffled some files, and opened one with a story Zeke had submitted with his application.

"I followed some of the stuff you did back in Lincoln. Not bad, kid, but this town is not for the weak of heart. Don't worry, though. We'll toughen you up. This stuttering thing. You get rid of it, and we'll talk about going on the air like you told me you wanted. Zeke swallowed and nodded. Like he hadn't tried to kick it before? Like it hadn't been a problem all his life? But Zeke wanted to go on the air. The possibility of it was one of the reasons he took this job.

"Look, kid," Harvey replied, "I've got an idea for your first assignment. This famous faith healer Fernando Dollar lives in DC. There's been a lot of controversy about this guy. Some think he's preying on the community. Some think he's legit. Let's see if he can cure your stuttering on camera. I want you to get him to try to heal your stuttering. I'm not expecting you to be healed, mind you, but if he does, great. And if he doesn't, we will have exposed a fraud. Either way, it's a win-win. Why don't you take a camera crew over there and interview the guy? I'll have Sly go with you to do the on-air interview. You give him the questions."

"Real nice," Zeke whispered under his breath.

"I heard that," replied Harvey, "and there was no stuttering."

"S…s…s…sorry, sir," said Zeke, "but…but…but tha… tha…tha…that's definitely ex…ex…exploiting my disability.

"We use what we can, kid. Anyway, it's a win-win. By the way, Zeke, did you fill out the paperwork for your security clearance and White House press pass?"

"Ye...ye...yes, sir," replied Zeke.

"Stop with the sir stuff," Harvey replied. "If you want to impress me, write some good copy."

"No...no...no...no problem, Boss," Zeke replied.

"Look, kid, this is a fifty-thousand-watt, class-A all-news station. We blast the night skies, and people hear us down on the Mexican border. Furthermore, what's local news for DC is national news for the rest of the country. You made it to the big leagues, kid. Now, get out there and hit your first home run." Harvey sat at his desk and yelled for one of the other reporters in the bullpen. "Sly, get in here. I want you meet Zeke." As Sly moseyed in, Zeke loosened his tie. "Sly, meet Zeke Jackson. We're expecting big things from him. Show him around the station and then take him downstairs and help him put together a camera crew for an interview."

"Welcome aboard," Sly replied. "I'll show you around."

"Wha...wha...what did you say your last name was?" asked Zeke.

"McDonald, Sly McDonald." After they left Harvey's office, Sly looked at Zeke and said, "So not even here an hour and you already got an interview. That's hitting the ground running." Zeke couldn't tell if that was a compliment or a warning. Before leaving the bullpen, Sly showed Zeke his cubicle. "You'll be sitting in this cubicle, right next to me," Sly told him. As they walked down the hall, Sly pointed out the bathroom, the break room, and the copy room.

"When do we…we…we get to see the on-air studios?" Zeke asked.

"What's the difference, kid? Harvey's not gonna let you on air with that stuttering problem." Zeke clenched at the nasty comment but tried to overlook it. "Listen, kid. I don't mean to get off on the wrong foot," Sly said. "It's just that around here we don't mince words. People just say what's on their mind. No offense."

"N…n…none taken," replied Zeke, "but that's why I need to do this interview. This guy, Fer-Fer-Fernando Dollar, is a famous fai…fai…faith healer who liv…liv…lives in DC. Ma…ma…maybe he can heal me of this stut…stut…stut… stuttering problem."

"You really think so, kid?" Sly asked.

"I…I…I…I don't really believe it, but my m…m…m… mom totally believes this stuff. Harvey th…th…thinks it's worth a shot. Anyway, if…if he doesn't, then we…we…we… we…we've exposed him on camera."

"Well, everyone knows about Fernando Dollar," said Sly. "He's made a business out of fleecing the flock. Let's go get this fraud."

They walked down two flights of stairs to the basement.

"The camera crews stay downstairs with the equipment and the studios. They like to keep the equipment and studios in the basement because it's cooler," Sly said.

They walked over to a room where the video and audio guys hung out cleaning their equipment and prepping for the next mission when not supporting the live in-station broadcasts. Sly introduced Zeke to the engineering supervisor.

"John, this is Zeke. He's a newbie, and Harvey has asked him to interview televangelist Fernando Dollar. Can you guys be ready tomorrow morning if Zeke lines up an interview?"

"Sure, I can spare two guys," John replied. "Are we gonna trap this fraud? My mom has been sending this guy money every month for the last five years. I'd sure like to bring him down."

"Sounds like you guys got a mission," said Sly. "Go get em, kid."

Suddenly, Sly's phone rang. It was Harvey. "Are you guys done down there? What's taking you so long?"

"We were just talking to John. We'll wrap it up".

"Get back up here. I want to talk to you."

"OK, Boss," said Sly.

They both went back up to Harvey's office. "What's up, Boss?" Sly asked.

"Sly, I want to talk to you alone," said Harvey. After Zeke left Harvey's office, Sly closed the door, but Zeke's cubical was close enough to overhear the conversation, especially with Harvey's boisterous voice.

"Watch him," he overheard Harvey say. "Go with him. He's going to give you some questions to ask Dollar on air, but I want you to do the on-camera interview. We can't risk someone stammering and stuttering all over the air."

"Sure thing, Boss," replied Sly.

Meanwhile, Zeke called the office of the Apostolic Reformed Church of which Fernando Dollar was the local pastor. The church secretary/assistant answered and listened to Zeke's request for healing from stuttering and an interview.

"Actually, Pastor Dollar has a healing session tomorrow morning with a small group of people," said the secretary. "I'll include you and let Pastor Dollar know. I'm sure it won't be a problem. Be here by ten am."

2

Slain in the Spirit

The next morning, Zeke climbed the steps to the station's front door with the same sense of confirmation but a new sense of urgency.

Boy, things move fast around here, he thought.

"Good morning, Zeke," said Julie as he entered the lobby.

"Goo…goo…good morning," Zeke replied. He wanted to talk more but couldn't muster the courage with his embarrassing stutter. The more he tried to impress someone, the worse it got.

I hope this guy can get rid of my stuttering, he thought, but Zeke didn't hold much hope for that.

"I heard you landed an interview with Fernando Dollar," said Julie. "Way to go."

"Th…th…thanks," replied Zeke.

Sly met Zeke downstairs with the camera crew. After loading the van, the four of them, Zeke, Sly, the cameraman, and the audio tech began their drive from Silver Spring, Maryland, to Capitol Heights, Maryland.

Sly commented, "We use the beltway whenever possible. DC is surrounded by Maryland and Virginia. Everyone calls it the DMV, the first letter of each state. A ten-mile drive can take hours in bad traffic." After about forty minutes, the camera crew along with Zeke and Sly arrived at the Apostolic Reformed Church.

"We made good time," said Sly. As they pulled into the parking lot, Sly commented, "This isn't a church. It's a campus. You don't make this kind of money off a pastor's salary."

"Is this you…you…your first time meeting a televangelist?" asked Zeke as he handed Sly a list of questions to ask Pastor Dollar.

"Well, I've never met one up close and personal," replied Sly.

"Well, I…I…I have," said Zeke. "Let me wa…wa…wa… warn you, this is gonna seem a little strange, so just go along and fo…fo…follow my lead."

Zeke, Sly, the cameraman, and audio tech unloaded the van and entered by way of the main entrance.

"He…he…hello," said Zeke to the receptionist. "We… we…we have an appointment to see…see…see Fernando Dollar. I'm Zeke Jackson, and this is Sly McDonald. We're… we're…we're from WJOP, and these other guys are our camera crew."

"Pastor Dollar is expecting you," said the receptionist. "Put on these badges and sign in, and security will escort you to Pastor Dollar's office."

As they were escorted to the office, they could not help but notice one hallway leading to a TV studio and another leading to an auditorium. Sly asked the security escort if they could glance inside the TV studio. He said yes and opened the studio door for a quick look.

"Three Sony PMW cameras," the cameraman yelled.

"What's a Sony PMW camera?" Zeke asked.

"It's an eighty-thousand-dollar studio camera capable of big screen, motion picture quality video," replied the cameraman. "Now, I know where to send my résumé."

After arriving at Pastor Dollar's office, the security officer introduced them to Fernando Dollar.

"Welcome to Apostolic Reformed Church," said Pastor Dollar. "What can I do for you gentlemen?"

"Well," said Zeke, "I have this stut…stutt…stutter I need to ge…ge…get rid of in or…or…order to broadcast new… new…news on the a…a…air. I ju…ju…just started this… this…this job yesterday, but I need to lose the sutt…stutt… stuttering."

"Well, why did they hire you in the first place?" asked Pastor Dollar.

"Har…Har…Harvey Schmidt, WJOP's new…new…news director, li…li…likes my reporting. He sa…sa…said I need to ge…ge…get rid of the stuttering if I want to g…g…go on the air and I do."

"Zeke, I don't think that's gonna be a problem. No, not a problem at all."

"But, don't you have to have faith?" asked Zeke.

"Well, yes, you do. Why? Do you not believe?" asked Pastor Dollar.

"Not really," replied Zeke.

"Not even a little?" asked Pastor Dollar.

"Maybe a little," said Zeke.

"Well, now, that's all you need. Jesus said, 'If you have faith as of a mustard seed, you shall say to this mountain, 'Move from here to there,' and it shall move,' and that's good enough for me," said Pastor Dollar. "So, boys, is that all you need?"

"We'd also like to ask you some questions about your ministry," said Sly. "Would you mind signing this waiver so that we can air the interview?"

"No problem. The media is always very skeptical of what I do and tries to discredit me, but my miracles always end up increasing people's faith. That's why I am still here and doing fine. Glory be to God. What's your question?"

The cameraman began shooting the interview. "Sly here will be doing the interview," said Zeke.

"Well, Pastor Dollar, do you really have the gift of healing?" asked Sly."

"Of course, I do," replied Pastor Dollar. "How do you think I built all this? Anyway. You'll find out in a few minutes, won't you, Zeke?"

"How much seed money did you take in last year?"

"How do you expect me to know that?" asked Pastor Dollar. "I'm doing God's work here. The money just comes. I don't count it. I'm not in this for the money. You'd have to talk to our accountants."

"Accountants plural?" Sly asked.

"Yes, we have several accountants and lawyers," replied Dollar. "Any ministry this size needs accountants and lawyers plural to handle its affairs."

"One last question," said Sly. "What's your annual salary?"

"Son," said Pastor Dollar. "Didn't your momma teach you any manners? You shouldn't ask people such personal questions even if you are a reporter. I don't even tell my congregation that kind of personal information. But, just to show you and the media that I'm above reproach, I'll tell you. I personally receive one hundred thousand dollars a year from this ministry. And, let me tell ya, that's not a lot money for Washington DC. Now, let's move to the auditorium. There's a group of parishioners waiting for services to begin," said Pastor Dollar.

As they entered the auditorium, they heard mesmerizing music. The auditorium was dark except for the flashing stage lights. Smoke billowed from beneath the stage.

"This is not like any church I've ever been to," said Sly.

"I ta…ta…told you it was going to get a little crazy," said Zeke. "The…the…the show hasn't even started yet."

"Show? What do you mean show?" asked Sly.

"That…that…that's what they call the service," replied Zeke.

Pastor Dollar walked out onto the stage. There must've been a hundred people in the auditorium.

"You all come up here on, stage," said Pastor Dollar. About fifty people came up. There were some men dressed in suits assisting Pastor Dollar. They got behind the people and guided them closer to the pastor. Pastor Dollar waved his right hand and several people fell back as if they had been knocked down by some inexplicable force. Pastor Dollar waved his hand again and several more fell backward. His assistants moved in to catch them and break their fall.

"This is really weird," said Sly.

The pastor motioned to Zeke to get in front of him. Pastor Dollar waved his right arm one more time. Zeke felt a blast of air push him until he fell backward, but one of the attendants was able to break his fall. The attendant helped Zeke to his feet and brought him before Pastor Dollar. Zeke appeared to be in a stupor. The pastor lightly smacked the sides of Zeke's face.

"Speak to me boy," said Pastor Dollar.

"What happened?" asked Zeke.

"You've been healed my boy," said the pastor. "Glory be to God Almighty."

Zeke shook his head. The trance was wearing off. Zeke grasped the pastor's hand as if to shake it. He looked the pastor directly in the eye.

"You don't need to thank me, Zeke," said Pastor Dollar. "Glory be to God Almighty."

"Your stomach has grown obese, and your belt has broken," said Zeke.

"What? What are you talking about, son?" asked Pastor Dollar. The pastor looked down at his stomach. "Same old flat stomach, and my belt is intact. You're still reeling from the healing, son. You'll be OK."

Zeke, still holding the pastor's hand and still looking him intently in the eye, asked, "Did you really heal me?"

"No," said Pastor Dollar. "I merely hypnotized you."

"So, you really don't have the gift of healing?" asked Zeke.

"That's right," said Pastor Dollar.

"So, how much seed money did you take in last year?" asked Zeke.

"Twenty million," Pastor Dollar immediately replied.

"And what is your annual salary?"

"Half a million a year plus expenses."

Zeke pulled his hand away from the pastor and said, "This interview is over."

"What was that all about?" asked Pastor Dollar. "And did I just say what I think I said?"

"Yes, you did," said Sly, "and we got it on camera. Let's get out of here, boys. We can get this on the Six O'clock News."

"You can't air that," said Fernando Dollar.

"You agreed to it," said Sly. "Remember the release you signed in your office? Take it up with WJOP's lawyers."

Zeke, Sly, and the camera crew quickly gathered up the equipment and exited the auditorium. They made their way to the reception area and out the front door, loaded the equipment in the van, and raced out of the parking lot.

"Wow," said the audio tech. "What just happened?"

"I'll tell you what just happened," said the cameraman. "Zeke just took down televangelist Fernando Dollar with three questions, and he got rid of the stuttering. Never seen anything like it."

On the way back to the station, the camera crew could not stop talking about it. They pulled up to the loading dock in the back of the station. As they unloaded the camera equipment and talked to the other employees, the cameraman described it to his buddies.

"That was so surreal. Never seen anything like it. All smoke and mirrors, and then out of nowhere, he just takes the guy down."

John, the camera crew supervisor, came out to the loading dock to see what all the commotion was about.

"What's going on guys? What just happened?"

"You're not going to believe this," said the cameraman. "Zeke got healed of his stuttering and he took down Fernando Dollar."

"Well, that's not exactly right," said Zeke. "Fernando Dollar did not heal me of my stuttering. He hypnotized me. He admitted to it."

"Is that right?" asked John.

"And, that's not all," said Zeke. "He admitted to taking in twenty million in seed money last year."

"Are you kidding me?" asked John.

"It's all here on video" said Zeke.

"Let's get this up to Harvey right away," said John.

Zeke, Sly, and the cameraman took the video up to Harvey's office.

"Harvey," said Sly, "we got it."

"Got what?" asked Harvey.

"We got Fernando Dollar."

"What do you mean you've got Fernando Dollar?" asked Harvey.

"He's a fraud," said Zeke. "He admitted to not having the gift of healing and raking in twenty million dollars in seed money last year."

"Zeke, you're not stuttering," said Harvey. "He healed you?"

"No, he hypnotized me. He admitted to it. It's a common trick used by faith healers."

"And, you captured this on video?" asked Harvey.

"Yes, sir," replied Zeke.

"Let me see that video," said Harvey.

The cameraman put on the video, and they all watched it.

Zeke provided commentary. "Notice the mesmerizing music, smoke billowing from the floor, strobe lights. It's all part of the show. Faith healers typically use things like music, lights, smoke, and other environmental effects to mesmerize their flock. They're experts at generating hypnotic effects. It's all about creating the aura, the feeling. By the time Fernando Dollar comes on stage, the people are ready to be manipulated. People are easier to manipulate when they are in a crowd. Watch as Pastor Dollar waves his arm. Many fall back and are caught by the assistants. It's a combination of suggestion and hypnotism that causes them to fall. For those who do not fall, he repeats the hand waving motion, a suggestion, until they do.

"Then, there's the seed money. Not only does it fill the coffers of the faith healer, but it also creates an anticipation of healing and prosperity as a deserved reward for their faith. Then, he tells me to get in front of him, and he waves his arm. At this point, I'm caught in the effects of his hypnotic trance. I've got a lot riding on this so I want this to work. I fall back and am caught by an attendant. When I return to my feet, I speak without stuttering, but there is something I cannot explain."

"What is it?" asked Harvey.

"I'm seeing Pastor Dollar differently. I see him as obese and with his belt broken, but in reality, he is, physically, a very thin man. I tell him, but he thinks it's some residual effect from the healing. Also, I feel emboldened to confront him and ask him some questions. So, I grab his hand and look him in the eye, and then it happens."

"What happens?" asked Harvey.

"I've got a lock on him," replied Zeke. "It's like he can't get loose 'til he answers me, and he can't do anything but tell the truth.

Zeke continued to recite the encounter to Harvey.

"Incredible. It's absolutely incredible," said Harvey. "Zeke, write me some copy to cover the story, and we'll lead with this on the Six O'clock News."

"You got it, Boss," said Zeke.

"By the way, how do you know so much about this?" asked Harvey.

"The most excitement in Lincoln County, Nebraska, happens at tent revivals. Some of it's legit. Some of it's not. Learning to tell the difference is a hobby of mine."

"Well, that's going to come in real handy around DC," replied Harvey.

3

Going Viral

As Zeke went to his desk to write up the story, Harvey got on the phone and called down to the TV studio. "Send Melany up here as soon as she gets off the air."

Melany Delaney, WJOP's lead anchor, finished up her midday report and went upstairs to see Harvey.

"What's up, Boss?" asked Melany.

"I want you to review this video we have from Zeke Jackson's interview with Fernando Dollar."

"Zeke? Isn't he the new reporter you just hired?"

"That's right," replied Harvey. "He hit the ground running, too. Here, watch this video."

Melany took the video to a production room and watched. Then, she returned to Harvey's office. "Wow! Looks like Zeke took him down."

"I want you to lead with this on the Six O'clock News," said Harvey.

"It's sure to go viral," said Melany. "Fernando Dollar is one of the most prominent televangelists in the country."

"Zeke's writing up copy as we speak," said Harvey, "and if it's anything like the commentary he gave us of the video, sparks are gonna fly."

After about an hour, Zeke brought his story into Harvey's office. Harvey read it.

"Sly," Harvey shouted out into the bullpen, "Get in here. Here's Zeke's copy. Looks pretty good to me. Do an edit on it. Nothing major. Then, cue up our social media desk to generate some buzz for the story ahead of our Six O'clock News."

"Got it, Boss," said Sly. With Zeke still in Harvey's office, Sly said to Zeke under his breath, "Looks like I'm working for you, now, kid?"

Later that afternoon, Ellie, the lead on the social media desk, called Harvey to tell him the story was starting to go viral. "We got one million views on Facebook in the last four hours," said Ellie, "and the retweets are accelerating on Twitter.

By the time the Six O'clock News came on, a good buzz had already been brewing. WJOP's *Evening News at Six* had become a staple in DC, Maryland, and Virginia. It was the most watched TV news show for fifteen years running in the DMV. After the Six O'clock News aired, Harvey received a call from the station manager, Jim Browning, who complimented him on breaking the story and told him that the network had already contacted him.

"They want to air the story later tonight on the *Nightly News*," said Jim, "and they want the reporter who broke the story to be part of a network special they're doing on prosperity preachers."

"Is that right?" responded Harvey. "This thing's getting even more buzz than I expected. I gotta give this kid a raise, and he's only been here two days."

"What kid?" asked Jim.

"Zeke Jackson," Harvey replied. "I just hired him this week. Kid's got great news instincts. Says he's got some kind of truth-telling ability. I don't know if I buy all that, but hey, if he can prove it, we'll use it. Why not?"

"Well," said Jim. "Give him the good news, and tell him great job for me. Well done. Congrats to all."

Harvey yelled into the bullpen, "Zeke, get in here. Close the door," Harvey commanded as Zeke entered his office. "Look, Zeke, is this truth-telling ability of yours for real?"

"Oh, it's for real," said Zeke as he closed the door behind him.

"I've got to know firsthand," said Harvey. "Let's conduct a little test. I want you to force me to tell the truth. There's something I've been hiding. Extract it from me."

"OK," said Zeke. "Grasp my right hand, and look me in the eye." Zeke saw that Harvey's right eye is missing from its socket. "Harvey, your right eye is missing."

"What do you mean?" asked Harvey. "My right eye is fine."

"Harvey, is there something you're hiding from us?"

"Yes," replied Harvey.

"What is it?" asked Zeke.

"I'm having an affair with the receptionist."

"Julie Stokes?" asked Zeke.

"Yes, that's right," said Harvey.

"How long has it been going on?" asked Zeke.

"Two years," said Harvey.

"Harvey, are you married?"

"Yes, but my wife doesn't know about the affair."

Zeke pulled his hand away from Harvey. Harvey moved back with a look of surprise. "Did I really tell you all that?" asked Harvey.

"Yes," replied Zeke.

"Tell me you won't tell anybody about this," said Harvey.

"You have my word," replied Zeke.

"Zeke, I have a feeling that your life is going to become very different now."

"What do you mean?" asked Zeke.

"I just got a call from the station manager. The network contacted him. They're airing your interview tonight. Also, they want you to appear on a national TV special they're doing on prosperity preachers."

4

The Past Catches Up

Harvey called everyone together in the news bullpen. "I want to pass on congratulations from the station manager on the great job you all did on the Fernando Dollar interview. The interview is airing tonight on the *Nightly News* at eleven o'clock. Special congratulations go to Zeke Jackson who conducted this interview and has been asked to appear on a network special on prosperity preachers. Zeke, you've had an unbelievable first week."

Everyone started clapping. At first, Zeke's face turned red but then he smiled and grinned. He put two fingers in his mouth and blew out a loud whistle.

"Can I say something? I just want to say that it was a team effort. Thank you." Zeke returned to his desk and straightened up a little before getting ready to leave the station for the night.

Sly came over to Zeke's cubicle. "I guess congratulations are in order. First impressions are hard to shake. You made an incredible one on everyone. Enjoy it while it lasts, kid."

"Thanks," replied Zeke.

There it was again, thought Zeke. Was it a compliment or a warning?

"By the way, I'll let it slide this once since you're new, but don't ever steal an on-camera interview from me again," warned Sly with a grin.

Now that's definitely a warning, thought Zeke even though he said it with a grin. "Wouldn't think of it," said Zeke. "I'm just happy to be here. It's a real break for a kid from Nebraska."

"Don't forget it," said Sly.

"Have a good night," said Zeke as he got up from his cubical and headed to the stairs.

"You too, rookie."

The next morning, Zeke arrived at the station, walked up the long set of white stone steps, and entered the lobby with a newfound sense of confidence. This was the first time in his life that he could remember when he didn't have a stutter, and he felt free.

"Good morning, Julie," he said. "How's our beautiful receptionist this morning?"

"There's something different about you today, Zeke."

"That's right," he replied. "No stutter."

"Wow, that's great."

Without giving it a second thought, he blurted out, "Julie, can I take you to lunch today?"

"I don't know, Zeke. Let me think about it."

"Sure, no pressure."

Zeke proceeded upstairs. By the time he reached his cubical his desk phone rang. It was Julie. "Zeke, I would love to go to lunch with you."

He wondered what had made up her mind. "Great. I'll meet you downstairs at twelve noon," said Zeke.

"Just keep it on the down low" said Julie.

"No problem," replied Zeke.

Harvey stopped by his cube to tell him that network's airing of the interview the previous night generated thousands of emails, four million Facebook posts, and continually increasing retweets. It had to be some kind of record.

"By the way," said Harvey. "I'm promoting you to News Reporter II, and I'm authorizing you for on-camera reporting. This is the quickest I've ever promoted a reporter. You'll have the responsibility of proofing and editing copy for more junior reporters and all your stories will be given bylines. Also, anything you write for social media will be given your byline but the frequency and quality of your submissions will be expected to increase."

"I hope this doesn't put me at the same level as Sly," said Zeke.

"Don't worry kid. Sly is a News Reporter III," said Harvey. "But it took him five years to get there."

Zeke thanked Harvey but cringed at his next comment.

"The bar has just been raised around here, people," said Harvey. Zeke noticed Harvey looking in Sly's direction. "Also, Zeke, I want you to write a first-person feature story on coming to the big city. What's it like coming to the DMV from a place like Nebraska? Give it to me by the end of the day."

"No problem, Boss," replied Zeke.

Zeke's phone started vibrating. It was his mom calling.

"Joseph, we saw the interview on the national news. What in the world is going on? You totally disrespected that man of God, Fernando Dollar. I thought we taught you better than that. Fernando Dollar has healed many followers. He is not a fraud. How am I going to explain this to all my church friends?"

"Mom, he admitted to taking twenty million dollars in seed money last year alone," replied Zeke.

"A man of God doing the Lord's work, especially the work he's doing, is worth the money," said his mom. "I love you son, but what you did was a disgrace to the family and to yourself."

"I love you too, Mom. Can we talk about this later? I've got to go now. I 've got a story to write."

Zeke was just starting on his feature story when Sly spoke up from his cubical. "Congrats on your promotion," commented

Sly. I guess you're the new golden child. I remember those days. Relish it, kid. It won't last."

Zeke looked at his email. He cringed again when he saw an email from Harvey to the entire news department notifying them of his promotion and asking them to join in the congratulations. He looked over at Sly and saw him shaking his head as he looked at his computer.

He must've just read the email, thought Zeke.

Zeke tried not to make further eye contact but worked diligently on his feature story the rest of the morning.

At noon, Zeke discreetly made his way to the lobby to meet Julie.

"Ready for lunch?" asked Zeke.

"Yeah, let's get out of here," said Julie as she hurried out from behind the receptionist's desk. "Ummm, maybe we shouldn't walk out together."

"Oh, right," replied Zeke. "Keeping it on the down low. The red Toyota pickup truck in the second row is mine. I'll unlock it, and you can go out first and get in."

Zeke watched as Julie walked toward his truck. All this creeping around like he was supposed to be ashamed of what he was doing was not exactly what he had in mind.

Anyway, if someone should be ashamed it should be Harvey, he thought. *Cheating on his wife with a much younger woman.* Well, sneaking around would have to suffice for now.

Zeke watched Julie get into his truck. Then, he walked out to it. "How do you feel about Greek food?" Zeke asked Julie.

"I love Greek food."

"Good, then we'll go to The Big Greek Café on Georgia Ave." It was only a five-minute drive.

After they entered the restaurant and were seated, a waiter came by with a menu.

"Julie, how about this Trio Dip Sampler as an appetizer?"

"Three dips with grilled pita. Sounds good," said Julie. "I like pita bread."

"What would you like to drink?" asked the waiter.

Julie and Zeke both ordered bottled water. As they waited for the appetizer, Zeke asked, "So how long did you say you've been working at WJOP?"

"Three years," answered Julie.

"How do you like it?"

"It's OK. Harvey has been good to me. He has a gruff demeanor, but he's really a big teddy bear. Enough about work. Who's you're favorite music group?"

"I really like Steely Dan," replied Zeke.

"That's pretty sophisticated for a Cornhusker," said Julie.

"I might have Nebraska values, but I've got cosmopolitan tastes," laughed Zeke.

"Were you in the 4-H Club growing up?" asked Julie.

"Nope. My father tried to get me interested in it, but it wasn't my style. I was in jazz band. Oh, here's the appetizer."

"Can I take your entrée order?" asked the waiter.

"I'll have the chicken souvlaki platter," said Julie.

"Same for me," replied Zeke.

As they enjoyed the appetizer, Julie dug a little deeper into Zeke's Steely Dan obsession. "So, what's your favorite Steely Dan album?"

"*Kamakiriad*," said Zeke. "But it's not really a Steely Dan album."

"How so?" asked Julie.

"It's a creation of Donald Fagen, the lead Steely Dan singer. It's a group of songs about a mythical drive down the East Coast in a Volkswagen Karmann Ghia."

"Kind of retro, isn't it?" asked Julie.

"I guess so," admitted Zeke. "But, it's good stuff. My dad had some old albums lying around. Here comes the chicken souvlaki," said Zeke.

Zeke ate the whole thing, but Julie had to get a doggy bag.

"We better get back," said Julie.

Zeke got the check from the waiter and paid the bill.

On the way back to work Julie said, "Thanks. That was fun. We'll have to do it again sometime."

"Definitely," said Zeke.

Julie smiled.

When they got out of Zeke's truck, they walked into the building together.

Zeke returned to the bullpen upstairs and continued working on his story. It was a slow day. Several employees stopped by to congratulate him. Zeke noticed that every time someone stopped by Sly seemed to leave the bullpen.

Zeke spent the rest of the afternoon polishing up his story before taking it to Harvey.

Zeke retrieved his mail from his company mailbox and returned to his cubical. As he was shuffling through his mail Sly came over and couldn't help but notice the *AP Stylebook* with the name Joseph Black written in black magic marker on the cover. "Who's Joseph Black?" asked Sly

"What?" asked Zeke.

"Your *AP Stylebook* has the name Joseph Black. Who's Joseph Black?"

"That's me," replied Zeke. "I changed my name."

"This isn't Hollywood, kid. It's just a news station. You'll be lucky if they even know your name after two years."

"Hey, it's quittin' time. Let's go around the corner to Jake's Tavern. We'll celebrate your success here at WJOP. My treat," said Sly.

"OK," said Zeke.

The two left the building and walked around the corner to the tavern.

"Hey Sly," greeted the bartender as they entered.

"You come here often," asked Zeke.

"Often enough for the bartender to remember my drink," replied Sly.

The two sat at a table in the back corner with Sly facing the door. The waitress brought a beer over to Sly. "What's your pleasure," she asked Zeke.

"Do you have Stella on tap?" asked Zeke.

"Yes," she replied.

"I'll have a twenty ounce," replied Zeke.

"You got it," replied the waitress.

Zeke noticed that Sly only sipped on his beer until the waitress arrived with Zeke's Stella. "Do you boys want a menu?" she asked.

"Not right now, sweetheart," replied Sly. He raised his glass to Zeke. "Cheers to many more great stories together." They tapped their glasses together and then took a big gulp. "You know, I think we make a good team."

Zeke folded his arms and leaned back in his chair. "What makes you think that we would make a good team?"

"I really know this town. I know people. With my contacts and your special gift, we're dynamite."

Zeke unfolded his arms, leaned forward, and took several gulps of beer. "You've got a point."

"You bet I do," replied Sly as he motioned to the waitress. "Another one for my friend here."

The waitress brought another twenty-ounce to Zeke.

"Now, drink up," said Sly who continued to sip on his first beer. "Cheers to no stuttering." Sly raised his mug to Zeke. Zeke took several gulps. "Now that you no longer have that stuttering problem, I think, together, we can rock this town."

Zeke was two twenty-ounce beers in on an empty stomach before Sly asked the question. "So, Zeke, tell me. Why did you change your name?"

"I told you. It's a long story."

"We got time," said Sly. "Anyway, if we're going to be working closely together, I want to know where you're coming from, where your head is at."

"Look, I got into some trouble back in high school. I changed my name because of all the negative attention."

"What kind of trouble?" asked Sly.

"I called in a fake bomb scare to my high school to avoid taking a test. I was charged with the crime, but since I was a minor my record was expunged."

"Ooooh," said Sly. "That's a big one."

"Well, I'm not proud of it," replied Zeke. "As I've gotten older, I've felt worse about it."

"How old were you when you did it?" asked Sly.

"I was fourteen."

"That's pretty young," replied Sly.

"Yeah, that's why they expunged my record."

"So, how did the FBI respond when you told them?" asked Sly.

Zeke looked puzzled.

"You did put it on your SF-86, didn't you?"

"No, my lawyer back in Lincoln told me I didn't have to report it since my record was expunged. He said I'd never have to report it to an employer or credit agency."

Sly scratched his head. "That's interesting," he replied. "I don't think that applies to the SF-86."

"I think I'm gonna head home now," said Zeke.

"Do you want me to drive you home?" asked Sly.

"No, I'm OK," said Zeke.

As Zeke left the tavern, he noticed Sly talking to someone on his phone. Zeke headed to his truck while Sly stayed behind. As he walked, he pondered what Sly said about the expungement not applying to the SF-86. Could his lawyer have been wrong? He was satisfied with himself that he had told Sly only half of the story.

For a brief moment, Zeke had a prick of conscience about driving under the influence, but he managed to convince himself that he felt sober enough and his drive was very short. So, he decided to risk it.

The next morning, Zeke arrived at the station, feeling a little uneasy about the way he confided in Sly.

It's probably nothing, he thought.

Zeke ran into Sly in the break room as they both grabbed a morning coffee.

"Good morning Sly," said Zeke. "Our conversation last night. That was for your ears only."

"Don't worry kid," said Sly "Your secret is safe with me."

They both went to their respective desks in the bullpen. "Zeke, Sly," yelled Harvey. "Get in my office. Zeke, I want you to go over to the White House press briefing today with Sly. You'll need to pick up your White House press pass from the Capitol police. Sly, go with him to the Capitol Building to make sure he gets his press pass."

"No problem, Boss," replied Sly.

Sly and Zeke took a station van to drive to the Capitol Building. After pulling up, Sly and Zeke entered the main door and approached security. They went through the metal detectors before being directed to the basement for press pass pictures.

"My name is Zeke Jackson," Zeke told the officer.

The Capitol police officer pulled Zeke's file up on the computer. "You've been red flagged," said the officer. "There's no indication of what it's concerning. I can give you a temporary pass today, but you're going to have to straighten this out before I can give you a permanent pass. Contact the FBI Clearance Investigation Department when you get back to your office."

Zeke got his temporary pass, and he and Sly drove over to the White House. After making it past the guardhouse, they parked the van and proceeded to the East Room for the briefing.

Once they entered the press room, they saw that there were fewer people in attendance than normal, so, they made their way up closer to the podium.

The White House Press Secretary, Bonnie Jenkins, made her way to the podium. "Good afternoon, ladies and gentlemen," said Madame Press Secretary. "As you know the fight in Afghanistan against the Taliban has been long and hard. We had some early success but are now looking at a resurgence of Al-Queda with the assistance of the Taliban. American troops have been incredible in eliminating many of the leaders of the Taliban and Al-Queda over the years, but the fight is not over and our troops are growing weary. With that in mind the president and vice president have decided to take a trip to Afghanistan. They will be meeting with the president of Afghanistan and the U.S. Army commander general to discuss future draw down of U.S. troops. I'll take questions now. Let's start off with a question from WJOP."

Sly spoke up, "Madame Press Secretary, are you concerned for their safety over there with the renewed fighting?"

"One of the purposes of the trip is for morale building for the troops. And, while we are always concerned about the safety of the president and vice president, we are not overly concerned with their safety on this trip. "

"Madame Press Secretary," said Zeke."

"Can you state your name, sir?" asked the press secretary.

"My name is Zeke Jackson, and I'm with WJOP," replied Zeke. "Madame Press Secretary, I don't mean to question your concern for the safety of the president and vice president; however, considering that latest incident where five Marine helicopters were shot down killing twenty crew members, I would think that you would not want to put the president and the vice president in harm's way."

"Zeke, I applaud you and the rest of the citizens out there for your concern for our president and vice president; however, I can assure you that their safety is our first concern."

Security Operations Commander General Hartack, who was standing behind the press secretary, tapped her on the shoulder and asked if he could address the question. "Zeke, as the general in charge of arranging for that trip from a military perspective, let me also re-assure you that the safety of the president and vice president is our first concern. In addition, the Secret Service will be totally involved in the planning of the trip, and we will consult daily with our intelligence in that area."

"Thank you," replied Zeke.

"By the way, Zeke, that was a very impressive interview you had the other day. I'd like to talk to you after the press conference if you don't mind."

"Yes, sir," said Zeke. "Thank you, sir."

After the press conference, the general approached Zeke, "Son, like I said, that was very impressive. Now, let me ask you straightaway, do you have some psychic ability to discern whether people are telling the truth, because that's what I got out of that interview?"

"Yes, but I wouldn't call it psychic," replied Zeke. "I don't know what it is or why I have it. I don't understand it. I mean, I don't really believe in that psychic stuff and I'm not very religious. I don't even go to church. I'm familiar with church and these faith healers because my mom and dad took me to church as a kid. But after I graduated high school I stopped going, and I really didn't believe anything. Also, I think a lot of these faith healers are really just frauds. Fernando Dollar is one of them."

"Well," said General Hartack. "I think you showed us that in the interview."

"I can prove it to you," said Zeke.

"Prove what," asked the general.

"That I have the ability to uncover truth," replied Zeke.

"I believe you, son. You don't have to prove anything to me."

Zeke extended his hand to the general for a handshake, but the general did not extend his hand. "Pardon me for not shaking your hand, son, but I'm a bit of a germaphobe. Pleasure to have met you, though."

Zeke didn't really buy the general's germaphobe excuse.

"Zeke, I don't think there's any more we can do here. Let's get out of here," said Sly.

"OK," replied Zeke.

Zeke and Sly left the East Room and went back to their van for the drive back to the studio.

"I think I'm gonna need to get back here and get some contact with people," said Zeke. "Do some more digging."

"'You're gonna need to get your press pass straightened out," said Sly.

"Yeah, a red flag. I wonder what that's all about," said Zeke.

When they returned to WJOP, Zeke went up to the bullpen only to hear Harvey call out, "Zeke get in here." Zeke went into Harvey's office, and Harvey told him to shut the door.

"Anything wrong?" asked Zeke.

"I just got a call from the FBI," said Harvey, "and they want to talk to you about your press pass and clearance. I told them to come over around two pm."

"That's fine," said Zeke.

"Anything you want to tell me, kid?"

"No, no," said Zeke. "Just that at the Capitol Building when I went to get my press pass, they would only give me a temporary one for the day because they said my file had a red flag on it."

"Why's that?" asked Harvey.

"I don't know," replied Zeke.

"Look, kid, don't be messing around with the FBI. You can get in deep doo-doo."

"Yes, sir," said Zeke.

Zeke left Harvey's office and returned to his cubicle in the bullpen. He sat at his desk wondering what the FBI had on him.

It must be the alias, he thought. *I guess I'm going to have to explain it to them. It happened when I was underage. They expunged my record.* He wondered how they found out.

As Zeke tried to figure out how they knew, Julie, called him on his desk phone. "Zeke, Agent Harry Jones from the FBI is here to see you."

"I'll be right there, Julie," said Zeke.

Zeke walked down to the reception area on the first floor trying to anticipate questions and contemplating what he was going to say.

When Zeke arrived at the front desk, Julie introduced him. "Mr. Jones, this is Zeke Jackson."

"Joseph Black, alias Zeke Jackson?" asked the FBI investigator. Julie frowned.

"I'll explain later," said Zeke, glancing at Julie.

"This is my assistant, Abby Sorensen," said Mr. Jones."

"Julie, can we use this conference room?" Zeke asked.

"Sure, I'll mark it as in use in Outlook. You won't be disturbed," said Julie. Zeke led them to the conference room.

"So, Mr. Jones, how can I help you?"

"Zeke, why did you change your name?" asked Mr. Jones. "I warn you, son, be careful what you say. Be truthful with us. You have not been entirely candid so far."

"OK, back in high school I called in a fictitious bomb scare to avoid taking a test. The school found out that I did it and expelled me for two weeks."

"Were you charged with the commission of a crime?" asked the FBI investigator.

"Yes," replied Zeke, "but since I was a minor and nothing like this ever happened before, my record was expunged, and everything was forgiven and forgotten. The people of Lincoln County, Nebraska, are very gracious, generous, forgiving people. They were extremely merciful and gracious to me. My lawyer told me that I'd never have to report it to an employer or on a credit check."

"That may be so, but you still have to report it to us," said Agent Jones. "The SF-86 is different. You have to list it. You might want to talk to a lawyer in the DMV. They're much more knowledgeable about clearance stuff than those Nebraska Cornhuskers. I think they're called Security Clearance Attorneys. Clearances are the life blood of the DMV. They can plead your case. You were given bad counsel."

Abby pulled Zeke's file out of her bag. "Zeke," said Abby, "I see you were in the military."

"Yes," said Zeke. "I did two years in the Marines after high school."

"Did you have a clearance in the Marines?" asked Abby.

"No," replied Zeke. "I didn't need one. I mostly did public relations work for the Marines. When I got out, I went to University of Nebraska for four years majoring in journalism."

"So you're twenty-five, right?" asked Abby.

"Yes," replied Zeke.

"Still a kid in my book," said Harry. "Look, kid, the agency has suspended your clearance for now. You're very lucky, kid. They could have charged you with a felony. Title Eighteen, lying to the FBI in a security investigation. I'm going to take this back to them, and see what they say. I know you're new here at the station and need the White House press pass and the clearance to do your job. You're also very young and stupid, if you ask me. So, keep your nose clean, and stay out of trouble."

"Do you think they will unsuspend my clearance? asked Zeke.

"It doesn't' look good, kid," said Harry. "The agency doesn't like it when you hide stuff from them."

"By the way, how did you find out my real name?" asked Zeke.

"That's a no brainer, kid. It was on your SF-86 but we didn't know why until yesterday," said Harry.

"What do you mean?" asked Zeke.

"We don't care that you changed your name, but we do care if you changed your name to cover up a past crime. We got a tip," said Harry. "Someone, here, from this station called in on the whistleblower line. You must've stepped on somebody's toes here, pretty bad. Take care, kid, and watch your back. This ain't Nebraska."

Zeke walked the FBI investigators to the front door. As they were leaving, Abby looked back at Zeke and smiled.

"Well, Zeke, she's pretty cute. Did you see the way she looked at you?" asked Julie.

"No, not really," replied Zeke.

"Well, I better go up and see Harvey." As Zeke walked up the stairs, he thought about the advice Agent Jones had given him. He decided he should take the advice and get an appointment with a Security Clearance Attorney.

As the two FBI investigators walked toward their vehicle, Harry commented, "That kid is a bit of a country bumpkin."

Abby responded, "He may be from Nebraska but he's no country bumpkin. Did you see that interview he did with Fernando Dollar?"

"No, I didn't see it," replied Harry."

"That kid is a pro," said Abby. "He took that guy down with three questions. Reporters with twenty years of experience have been trying to do that for years."

Meanwhile, Zeke went back upstairs to talk to Harvey. When Zeke arrived at Harvey's office, he saw Sly talking to him. Zeke knocked softly on the door.

"Come in," said Harvey. Zeke entered.

"So, I hear you had a talk with the FBI. Did you get your clearance straightened out?" asked Sly.

Zeke gave Sly a stern look.

"Sly, I need to talk to Zeke alone. Close the door behind you. So, Zeke, what's going on?" asked Harvey.

"The FBI suspended my clearance."

"Why?" asked Harvey.

"They found out about a crime I committed in high school." Zeke filled Harvey in on what happened.

"And, you didn't tell the FBI this on the original SF 86?" asked Harvey.

"No, my lawyer back in Lincoln told me I didn't have to disclose it, but I guess it's different when it comes to the FBI."

"That's kind of stupid," said Harvey. "Stupid Cornhusker lawyers."

"Yeah, that's what the FBI investigator said."

"Is the FBI gonna unsuspend your clearance and press pass?" asked Harvey.

"I don't know," said Zeke. "It doesn't look good."

"Well, I guess I can keep you on for the time being, but it's going to be really hard for you to report news in DC without a press pass," said Harvey. "I guess I can have you editing copy, writing feature stories, and helping the social media group with stories."

Zeke shook his head and rubbed the back of his neck. "I can't believe this is happening," he said.

"Look, kid, don't worry about that for now. I've got something else for you," said Harvey. "The network has decided to go ahead with that special on prosperity preachers, and they want you to be part of it. After watching your interview of Fernando Dollar and becoming aware of your familiarity with televangelists and faith healers, they thought you'd be a good addition to the special."

"How did they know about my exposure to faith healers and televangelists?" asked Zeke.

"Well, kid, I told them. I've been known to brag about my staff from time to time. It's called tooting your horn."

"Well, thanks, I guess," said Zeke.

"They're going to do it on the Jack Cong show," said Harvey. "As you probably know, it's the most watched nightly talk show in the country with over two million nightly viewers. Jack has interviewed some of the most prominent people in the world. This is a wonderful opportunity for you. It'll put you on the world stage. Whatever you say or do on the show will be remembered and can be replayed years from now. So, be careful, but be bold. Just follow Jack's lead. He's been at this several years. He knows what he's doing. The show airs tomorrow night at eight pm. I'll have Julie make airline reservations from National to JFK and a hotel reservation for you. You'll need to be on set by three pm for makeup and preparations. They'll have dinner brought in and catered. So, have fun. Enjoy."

"Thanks. I'll try," said Zeke.

Zeke left Harvey's office and slowly walked back to his cubicle pondering a couple of things. He was worried about his clearance. He was also worried about this gift or supernatural ability that he had. Would it last forever or was it temporary, and was it really a gift from God? He just didn't understand it. It was really weird. He decided to call his aunt to talk to her about it. She had always been interested in his spiritual well-being and had a deep abiding faith in God.

Zeke called his Aunt Becky, and she answered. "Joseph, it's wonderful to hear from you," said Aunt Becky. "So, how are you doing?"

"Well, I'm not stuttering anymore," said Zeke. "Did you see the interview I did with Fernando Dollar?"

"Yes, I saw it," said Aunt Becky. "Your mom and dad called me complaining of how disappointed they are in you."

"Yeah, they're so worried about what their friends think. They don't stop to question what's really going on. I just can't blindly accept everything on face value like they do."

"Look, Joseph, you may be right about Fernando Dollar. Not every shepherd is a true shepherd. The Bible tells us to test the spirits to see if they be in the faith. There are many wolves out there preying on the sheep. You may very well have discovered one. But the real question is, what is going on with you?"

"Well, Aunt Becky, that's what I called you to talk about. I don't know. I mean, I don't understand. This Fernando Dollar hypnotizes me to get rid of the stuttering, and the stuttering goes away but I'm left with this seemingly supernatural ability which I can't even believe I have. But I do have it and I can prove it. It's so weird. But I don't even want it. I don't know how to get rid of it. Is it a gift from God? Is it a plague for something I've done wrong? Why do I have this thing? And, besides that, someone in my office is out to get me, and I just lost my security clearance."

"What do you mean?" asked Aunt Becky.

"The FBI found out about the bomb scare in high school.

"Didn't you tell them when you filled out the security application?" asked Aunt Becky.

"No, the lawyer said I didn't have to put it on applications. I think my coworker reported it to the FBI on the whistleblower line. It feels like my life is careening down the highway at one hundred miles per hour."

"You know, Joseph, when you were a baby, we had you dedicated to the Lord at the Holiness Pentecostal Church. A man came up to your mother, father, and me and told us that God was going to use you in a very special way. I think he was a prophet. We call these type of people prophets at our church because we believe they have the gift of prophecy. The man did not elaborate, but this could be the fulfillment of his prophecy. Joseph, have you thought about committing your life to the Lord?"

"I'm not ready for all of that," Zeke replied.

"Joseph, life is too complicated and comes at you too fast to rely on your own instincts. Not to mention being able to tell the wolves from the sheep. You need the Lord to guide you. Promise me you'll think about it?"

"OK, Aunt Becky, I'll definitely think about what you said. Oh, by the way, I'll be on the *Jack Cong* show tomorrow night. He's doing a special on prosperity preachers and the network wants me on it because of the Fernando Dollar interview."

"I'll watch and I'll be praying for you," said Aunt Becky. "All my love."

"Me too, and thanks. You've always been someone I can talk to, "said Zeke.

After getting off the phone with Aunt Becky, Julie called Zeke with his itinerary for the trip to New York.

"Zeke, I've got you on a redeye out of Reagan National on Southwest tomorrow morning. It was the best I could do on short notice. You'll be going to JFK. From there just take a cab to the CBS Studio in New York City. We'd rather you not be driving in New York. I booked you at the Roosevelt Hotel which is walkable from the studio. I'll send you the itinerary. Also, since you'll be there early, I scheduled you a tour of the set of *News This Morning*. I also scheduled you a brief meeting with the news director.

"Thanks, Julie. I think I'll head home now. I'll need to get to bed early to get to Reagan National for a six am flight. Plus, tomorrow is going to be a long day," said Zeke.

"Good luck, Zeke. I'm rooting for you," said Julie.

The next morning, Zeke drove to Reagan National Airport and parked his car in long-term parking.

This place is really busy, he thought. It took him twenty minutes to find a parking spot. He boarded the shuttle bus to the airport terminal and noticed several people staring at him.

Maybe it's my imagination, he thought.

After arriving at the Southwest terminal, he made his way to security and proceeded through the check-in line with everyone else. He showed the TSA officer his driver's license and boarding pass.

"Didn't I see you on TV recently?" asked the TSA officer.

"You probably did," said Zeke. "I work for WJOP."

"Fernando Dollar interview, right?"

"That's right," said Zeke.

"Have a nice flight," said the TSA officer.

This place is like a small town, Zeke thought. *Everybody knows me.*

As Zeke made his way through the airport to his gate, again he noticed several people staring at him. One rather stately gentleman even motioned to him with what seemed like a halfhearted two finger salute. Zeke boarded the plane for a rather uneventful forty-five-minute flight to JFK, except for the occasional stare. After the plane landed, Zeke got a cab to CBS headquarters in Midtown New York. During the thirty-minute drive the cabbie engaged Zeke in conversation.

"Didn't I just see you on TV?" asked the cabbie.

"I work for WJOP, a CBS affiliate in DC," Zeke replied. "Seems like a lot of people recognize me. I did an interview with the televangelist Fernando Dollar."

"Right. That was good," said the Cabbie. "You really took that guy down."

"Well, I'm going to be on the *Jack Cong* show tonight. Jack's doing a special on prosperity preachers."

"Well, if you think people recognize you now, wait until tomorrow. Well, here you are kid, CBS headquarters. Good luck."

"Thanks," said Zeke.

Zeke approached the tall black marble building, commonly called BlackRock, and walked into the lobby. He approached the reception desk. "Hello, I'm Zeke Jackson from CBS affiliate WJOP in DC."

"Welcome to New York," said the receptionist. "We were expecting you. Why don't you sign in and get a temp badge, and you can go upstairs and get settled in, and your page can show you around the facility."

"Sounds good," replied Zeke. "Can't wait to see the home of David Letterman." After Zeke checked in, a page came over to accompany him.

"I think my assistant scheduled me for a tour of the *News This Morning* set," said Zeke.

"Yes," said the page. "I have your schedule. It's time for your tour of that set. I'll take you right up. Within minutes, Zeke was on the set of *News This Morning*, which was live on the air. After the show cut to a commercial break, co-host Anthony Lakeland spotted Zeke and motioned for him to come over.

"Zeke Jackson, right?"

"Yes, that's right, but how do you know my name?"

"Are you kidding me?" asked Mr. Lakeland. "You're famous around here. Everyone loves that interview you did with Fernando Dollar. I hear you're making an appearance today on Jack Cong. Look, I've got to go, but I'll be sure to watch you tonight. Nice to have met you. Good luck."

"Thanks," replied Zeke.

After talking with Anthony Lakeland, the page escorted Zeke to the cafeteria for lunch. Zeke stayed in the cafeteria for a few hours, alone with his thoughts.

Where was all this leading? he thought. After all, all he really wanted to do was report the news. Somehow, he felt he was starting to become it. After lunch his page showed up with his itinerary.

"Mr. Jackson, I have you scheduled for a meeting with the news division president, Jamie Gerrard," said the page. "Let's head upstairs."

The page escorted Zeke upstairs to the news director's floor. When they arrived, the page told the receptionist that Mr. Zeke Jackson was here for his appointment with Miss Gerrard. The page introduced Zeke Jackson as the news reporter from CBS affiliate WJOP in DC who interviewed Fernando Dollar. "I'll check to see if she's ready to see you," replied the receptionist. The receptionist paged Miss Gerrard.

"Yes, Judy?" Miss Gerrard replied.

"Are you ready for your appointment with Zeke Jackson? He's the news reporter from CBS affiliate WJOP in DC."

"Yes, send him in."

"Zeke, just knock on the door and go ahead in," said the receptionist. Zeke hesitated. It seemed like an apartment, not an office.

"Hi, Zeke," said Miss Gerrard. "Thank you for agreeing to go on the *Jack Cong* show."

"Pleasure to meet you, Miss Gerrard. Harvey Schmidt sends his regards."

"Harvey and I go way back to journalism school at Columbia University," said Miss Gerrard.

"Harvey hired me at WJOP."

"He certainly has a knack for hiring good people," said Miss Gerrard. "You've really taken that station by storm so far. Congratulations and keep up the good work. I look forward to seeing you on the *Jack Cong* show when it airs tonight. Now, Zeke, if you'll excuse me, I must get back to it. By the way it's about time for you to be on set."

"Very nice to have met you, Miss Gerrard."

After leaving her office, Zeke and the page thanked the receptionist. "It's about that time," said the page "I need to get you up to the set of the *Jack Cong* show."

As Zeke walked on to the set of the show, he was greeted by the floor manager.

"Zeke Jackson?" asked the floor manager.

"Yes, that's me."

"Oh, good. I was hoping you would arrive a little early. Jack wants to talk to you. I'll introduce you." They walked over to Jack's dressing room. "Jack, this is Zeke Jackson."

"Zeke, pleasure to meet you. It's going to be a great show tonight. Look, I saw your interview with Fernando Dollar, and I was very impressed. You seem to have quite a bit of knowledge about faith healers and the whole prosperity preacher thing. Don't worry about a thing. Just follow my lead, and we'll give them a great show. I'm going to want to demonstrate your special ability by having you perform it on me. I don't want to discuss it beforehand because I don't want it to come off rehearsed. But I just wanted to give you a heads up."

"What if you say something that you don't want aired?" asked Zeke.

"Well, we can edit it out," replied Jack.

Zeke hung around the studio until it was time for the show. Finally, he heard the floor manager say, "Everyone on set." Once Zeke and Jack were in position, the floor manager gave the countdown. "Five. Four. Three. Two. One." The red light on the camera directed at Jack came on.

"Good evening, ladies and gentlemen. We have a very interesting show for you tonight. The subject for tonight's show is prosperity preachers. For those of you not familiar with the term, a prosperity preacher is someone who promotes the idea that health and wealth are the product of faith in God. Prosperity preachers state that the believing and trusting servant of God should, in fact, expect health and prosperity. There are many prosperity gospel preachers across America. However, I am not going to name them. From time to time, we've had them on the show. Tonight, however, we have a very special guest, our very own Zeke Jackson from our CBS affiliate WJOP in Washington, DC. Recently, you may have seen Zeke's interview with televangelist Fernando Dollar, a prominent prosperity preacher headquartered in DC. Zeke, welcome to New York and the *Jack Cong* show. Tell us a little about yourself and your experience with Fernando Dollar."

"Thank you, Jack. It's great to be in New York City and on your show. New York is a far cry from my home state of Nebraska. I very recently came to work for WJOP in DC. Before that I was working for CBS affiliate, KOLN, in Lincoln, Nebraska. Harvey Schmidt, the news director at WJOP, offered me a job as a news reporter. My background was in news writing and investigative reporting. I had a speech impediment, a stuttering problem, which prevented me from going on air. Fernando Dollar healed me of the stuttering problem; however, he did not really heal me. He hypnotized me and admitted to it in the interview. Fernando Dollar is a very wealthy man and this year alone he has admittedly taken in twenty million dollars in seed money."

"Now, Zeke, I understand that you have a special gift. Can you explain a little bit about that gift?"

"Sure. Fernando Dollar used what faith healers refer to as 'slaying in the spirit'. In most cases, this is a hypnotic technique. Fernando Dollar is very good at it. When I awoke from the hypnosis, I discovered that I had the ability to see people's spiritual condition manifested in a physical form. In the case of Fernando Dollar, he is a very thin man. When he extended his hand to help me and I grabbed it while looking him in the eye, I saw him as obese to the point where his belt was broken. I believe this was a reference to the area of truth or lack thereof in his life. I felt a prompting to ask him the same questions that we had asked him earlier in his office. One was, do you have the ability to heal? He said no and told me that he hypnotized me to remove my stuttering. Then, I asked him how much seed money he had taken in last year. He immediately replied, twenty million dollars. Before, he was not willing to divulge this. Then, I pulled my hand away and, instantly, he realized what he had said."

"Have you had this experience with anyone else?" asked Jack.

"Yes," said Zeke. "One other person, but I'd rather not say who."

"Would you be willing to try this on me, right now on the air?" asked Jack.

"Yes, I could do that," replied Zeke.

"We're going to commercial," said Jack. "When we come back, I'll reveal what I want Zeke to ask me."

After four minutes, they were ready to return. The floor manager counted them in motioning with his hands. Two fingers, one finger. He pointed at Jack to indicate he was recording.

"We're back, and with me, I have Zeke Jackson. In a minute, I'm going to be asking Zeke to demonstrate his special gift on me. Zeke, I've been doing the *Jack Cong* show for the last ten years. I've been very open with my life and very honest with my audience, and they have rewarded me with their loyalty to my show. But, a few years ago something changed in my life which I thought I should tell my audience. However, I've been reluctant to do so for fear of losing viewership. Tonight, I am asking Zeke, to use his special gift to extract this information from me. Zeke, tell me what to do."

"Jack, are you sure you want to do this?"

"Yes," said Jack," let's do it."

"OK," replied Zeke. "Take my right hand like you're going to shake it and maintain a firm grasp and look me firmly in the eye."

Jack followed Zeke's instructions. Zeke's saw Jack in the spirit. Jack appeared to be coughing uncontrollably.

"Are you okay?" asked Zeke.

"Yes, I'm fine," replied Jack.

"You're not coughing?" asked Zeke.

"No, not at all. Why? What do you see?" asked Jack.

"I'll explain later," said Zeke. "Jack, what is it that you've been hiding from your audience?"

"Two years ago, I had an affair with a young lady on my staff which resulted in a pregnancy. From this affair, I have a two-year-old son who I have been supporting."

"Jack, do your wife and family know this?"

"No, they do not," Jack replied. Zeke noticed that the coughing stopped, and he let go of Jack's hand.

"What just happened?" Jack asked. "Did I just admit to having an affair?"

"Yes," Zeke replied.

"Oh boy," Jack said. "My wife will be devastated. Zeke, what was all the coughing that you thought you saw?"

"I was seeing your spiritual condition," Zeke explained. "The coughing indicated something you were trying to get out that kept bothering you. After you told us, the coughing stopped. Eventually, this spiritual condition would have manifested in a physical ailment of some sort."

"Thank you, I guess," said Jack. "I'm not sure what to say. I could never have admitted that on my own, but now I have a huge mess to cleanup."

"Jack, I think you did the right thing in admitting it. It would have eventually come out anyway. Your audience loves you. I don't think they're going to hold this against you. The real cleanup work will be with your family, especially your wife."

"Zeke, Fernando Dollar may be a fraud, but I think you're the real deal. Folks, we'll be right back after this commercial."

The floor manager motioned to Jack. "This is sure to get people tuning into the show by the tens of thousands," said the floor manager.

After four minutes, they were ready to return. The floor manager counted them in again motioning with his hands. Two, one. He pointed at Jack to indicate he was recording.

"We're back, and with me I have Zeke Jackson. Before commercial, I asked Zeke to demonstrate his special gift on me. If you did not see it, you can catch the replay at one am. Amazing, truly amazing. My next guest is from Oral Roberts University and is here to help us understand the concept of seed money by prosperity preachers today. Meanwhile, we'll say goodbye to Zeke. Zeke, thanks for coming on the show." Zeke went to shake Jack's hand. "Nope, not gonna do that again," Jack said. Instead, Jack gave him a fist pump.

Zeke walked off the set and went over to the page. They walked back to the green room where Zeke removed his jacket and tie and handed it to the page to give back to wardrobe. Zeke picked up his own jacket which he left there. The producer of the *Jack Cong* show, Jim Stelling, who was in the green room, congratulated Zeke on his performance on the show. Zeke ran his fingers through his hair and scratched the back of his head.

"Thanks," said Zeke. "But I don't feel very good about it. I'd feel a lot better if I hadn't caused Jack to spill his guts like that."

"Well, Jack is a TV veteran. He knows just how far to push things. Anyway, if there's something he doesn't want to air, we still have time to edit it out. I'll tell him that you're concerned for him."

"Thanks," said Zeke. "It's been a long day," said Zeke to the page. "Can you get me a cab to the Roosevelt Hotel?"

"Sure," said the page. "Let's go."

Zeke and the page took the elevator down to the lobby. They went out to the street, and the page hailed a cab.

"Goodbye, Mr. Jackson," said the page and then extended his hand to Zeke.

Zeke hesitated. He was exhausted. Then, he reciprocated with a fist pump.

"I'm a bit of a germaphobe," said Zeke.

"Right," said the page.

"Thanks for escorting me around today. Good luck in your career," said Zeke.

Zeke got in the cab. "Roosevelt Hotel, please," Zeke told the driver.

After arriving at the Roosevelt Hotel, Zeke payed his fare, grabbed his overnight bag, and checked in to his room. Facing another red-eye flight, Zeke quickly fell asleep. The next thing he heard was a 4:00 am alarm clock. Zeke got out of bed, washed up, and went to the lobby to hail a cab to JFK. He would grab a cup of coffee at the airport.

Not surprisingly, there was a cab in front of the hotel waiting for a fare. The doorman motioned to the cabbie to pull up.

"Hey, weren't you just on the *Jack Cong* show last night?" asked the doorman.

"Yes," replied Zeke.

"You're that guy who gets people to tell the truth, some kind of modern-day prophet."

"Is that what they're calling me now?" asked Zeke. "I'm just a news reporter. I'm no prophet."

Then, he opened the rear door and Zeke got in.

"JFK, please," Zeke told the cabbie.

"It'll take about thirty minutes this time of the morning," said the cabbie.

Zeke noticed a TV monitor in the cab containing news highlights. On it was the headline, "Jack Cong Reveals Love Child to Modern Day Prophet". Yes, it was a report on last night's show.

After the cabbie dropped him off at the Southwest terminal, Zeke checked in and went through security. Then, he stopped by a coffee shop. The cashier stared at him as he bought his morning coffee. He looked down at the newspaper rack, and realized why. His picture along with Jack Cong was on the front page of *Newsday*, the *New York Daily News*, and the *New York Post*, all popular, high circulation papers for New York. He did not purchase the papers to keep as a souvenir of his time in New York on the *Jack Cong* show. For the first time since moving to DC and taking the job at WJOP, he started to regret his decision. He didn't want to ruin people's lives. He didn't want to be known as a sleaze journalist. The gift, it had to be meant for something other than this. To Zeke, Lincoln County, Nebraska, was looking better every day.

Zeke went to his gate and boarded the plane for his flight back to DC. He noticed more and more people staring at him. The trip was a quick hour-long flight back to Reagan National Airport.

5

More Trouble with the FBI

After Zeke deboarded the plane, he took a shuttle to long term parking to pick up his car. When he arrived at the station, he saw Julie at the reception desk.

"Harvey wants to see you," she tells Zeke.

"OK. I'll go right up," said Zeke. As Zeke walked down the hall toward Harvey's office, Harvey saw him.

"Zeke, come on in here. I saw the show. That was quite a performance, kid. CBS headquarters is thrilled. Jack's viewership doubled during the time you appeared on his show. They're even talking about including you on some show on a permanent basis."

"Boss, we need to talk," said Zeke.

"Sure, kid," said Harvey. "What's on your mind?"

"I'm not sure about all this," said Zeke.

"What do you mean?"

"Well, I came here to *report* the news, not *be* it. More and more, I'm becoming the story. Yesterday was a perfect example."

"Zeke, don't you realize what an incredible position you're in? You haven't even been here a month, and the CBS network is considering you for a major network show. This would change your whole life. You're talking big money, fame and fortune, book deals. I'm salivating just thinking about it," said Harvey. "Let me tell you something, kid. I've been trying to get to CBS headquarters for the last five years. I was being considered for CBS News Division Director two years ago. I've got a lot of contacts at BlackRock headquarters. I could be a big help to you there and vice versa. Anyway, losing your security clearance is not exactly advancing your career around here. This is a government town, and you're not much good without a clearance and access to the inner sanctuaries of the White House, Pentagon, and State Department to name a few. Think about it hard, kid."

"Yeah, I'll do that," replied Zeke.

"Meanwhile, tell Sly I want to see him," said Harvey.

"Yes, Boss," said Zeke.

Zeke went to Sly's cubicle, seething over what Harvey said to him.

What a nasty guy, he thought.

"Boss wants to see you," he said to Sly.

"Heard you were a big hit at BlackRock," Sly replied. "Too bad about the clearance, though. Once the FBI thinks you're lying, it's impossible to convince them otherwise."

Oh, great, Zeke thought.

After Sly went into Harvey's office, Harvey told him to close the door.

"What's up, Boss?" asked Sly.

"Look, I know it hasn't been easy for you around here lately. I mean you've been here several years and you were pretty much my main reporter. Then, Zeke comes in and right away he becomes the star of the show. Gets promoted to News Reporter II after the first week."

"Yeah, well, I'll admit it's bugged me a little," replied Sly.

"Come on. Admit it. You were more than a little bugged."

"OK. I'll admit it. I was very angry."

"Angry enough to blow the whistle on Zeke?"

"How did you know that?" asked Sly.

"The FBI investigator told me that someone from WJOP reported an SF-86 discrepancy on Zeke Jackson. So, what exactly did you tell the FBI that caused them to suspend his clearance?" asked Harvey.

"I told them that he failed to disclose a crime he committed when he was in high school."

"How did you know that?" asked Harvey.

"He told me."

"What?" asked Harvey. "Why would he tell you that?"

"I oiled him up, and he spilled his guts," replied Sly as he snickered.

Harvey smiled. "That sounds like something I would do. I think I've trained you too well. What else did he tell you?"

"Not much," said Sly. "He was a minor, so his records were expunged."

"What did he do?" asked Harvey.

"He called a bomb scare into his high school. Looks like it was just a prank."

"Not the kind of prank the FBI likes to hear about," said Harvey. "But I sure would like to see that he doesn't get that clearance back."

"Why?" asked Sly. "I mean I know why I called the FBI whistleblower line. I didn't like the way he came in here and took over, but you hired him. Why would you not want him to succeed?"

"I do want him to succeed, but not here," said Harvey.

"Why not?" asked Sly.

"Because I want him to go to BlackRock and establish a career there. He's more good to me at headquarters than he is here. We'll have an inside man that can help us get things we want from headquarters."

"Look Boss. I can try to dig up some dirt on him. Since his records were expunged, I won't be able to find out any more info from the usual sources, but I could go to his hometown and high school and talk to people who have firsthand knowledge," said Sly.

"No, I expect the FBI will be making a trip to Lincoln, Nebraska seeing all the records have been expunged. Let's just leave it to them. I'll monitor the situation by talking with Zeke."

As Zeke saw Sly coming back to his desk, Zeke got a call on his cell and left his cubical to take it. It was his Aunt Becky.

"Aunt Becky?" answered Zeke.

"Joseph, I saw your interview with Jack Cong. That was amazing. You definitely have a prophetic gift."

Zeke shook his head and sighed. He was so tired of the whole thing.

"Well, that may be, but I don't want it. That's all people seem interested in. Let's watch Zeke make someone spill their guts. No thanks. If I can't get the truth out of people by honest investigating and reporting, then I don't deserve to get it. I don't want to get it by trickery."

"Joseph, it's not trickery. God gave you this gift. He must've had a reason for giving it to you. He wants you to have it and use it. Mark my words. He's gonna use this gift. There's gonna come a time and situation where God is gonna use this gift in a big way for something very good. You just stay the course and wait."

"OK, Aunt Becky. By the way, did Mom and Dad see it?" asked Zeke.

"Yeah, they called me," said Aunt Becky. "They wondered how you could do such a thing to that nice man, Jack Cong, and embarrass him, not to mention them."

"That figures," responded Zeke. They're always worrying about their image. "Look, Aunt Becky, I've gotta go. I'll talk to you later."

"Sure," said Aunt Becky. "Blessings on you."

Zeke returned to his desk.

FBI Agent Harry Jones pulled up to Lincoln High and got out of his rental on a Tuesday morning in early September. The parking lot was full. Kids were back in school. He entered the school's office and asked to speak to the principal, Mr. Jim Slaughterback.

"Hello, I'm Special Agent Harold Jones." He opened his suit jacket revealing his FBI badge attached to his belt. I'd like to speak with the principal."

"Have a seat, Mr. Jones. I'll tell Mr. Slaughterback. you're here to see him," said Rita Sykes, the school secretary. After she returned from the principal's office, she asked, "Would you like something to drink? A cup of coffee, perhaps?"

"No thanks. I just had a cup," said Harry. From his seat, Harry looked around the office. He spotted a football trophy on Mrs. Sykes's file cabinet. "Looks like you guys are pretty big in football."

"Oh, yes," replied Mrs. Sykes. "We were state champs last year. That trophy usually sits in our display case in the entrance hallway. Mr. Grosscamp, the P.E. teacher, asked me to get it out for him. Some pep speech he has in mind."

The principal walked out of his office, approached and greeted Agent Jones, "Hello, Agent Jones. How can I help you?"

"Pretty nice school you have here," said Agent Jones. "I need to talk to you about a former student, Joseph Black."

"Come into my office," said Principal Slaughterback. Agent Jones followed him into his office. "Have a seat, Agent Jones."

"Did he get into some kind of trouble?" asked the principal.

"No, not exactly," replied Agent Jones. "But he had his security clearance suspended for not reporting a prior incident at this high school. I was hoping you could tell me what happened."

"Well," asked Mr. Slaughterback, "can I see your badge?"

Agent Jones detached his badge from his belt and handed it to Principal Slaughterback who examined it and handed it back.

"I thought all of his records were expunged," said Principal Slaughterback.

"They were," replied Agent Jones. "Even the FBI has no record of them. He must've had some good lawyers, but Joseph Black recently applied for a security clearance. On the SF-86 clearance form, he made no mention of the fake bomb scare he was responsible for in high school. My assistant heard nothing about this when she did our initial investigation. I guess people either didn't know or, like you, figured his under-age records were off limits. We were notified of this by a whistleblower. That's why I'm here talking to you directly. I'm re-investigating his clearance. Now, Mr. Slaughterback, please tell me what happened the day of the bomb scare. I don't think I need to say this to a man in your position, but I will just so we're clear. I warn you, lying to or intentionally deceiving an FBI investigator is a felony."

"OK. OK," said Principal Slaughterback. "Two teachers died of heart attacks the day of the bomb scare. They didn't know it was fake. After I made the announcement, the teachers started escorting their classes out of the building. After they got them out, the two elderly teachers both collapsed with massive heart attacks, both of them. The police discovered that Joseph Black had called in the bomb scare. They didn't charge him with the teachers' deaths, but they could have. Joseph's lawyers talked them out of it, Joe being a minor and the teachers being lifelong, heavy smokers. Anyway, Joseph hadn't been trying to hurt anybody. He did it to get out of taking a test, a foolish prank. The authorities went very lenient on Joseph. They only charged him with the crime of reckless endangerment. He only did six months in juvie and was released to his parents on probation for a year. After that, Joseph's police record was expunged."

"Thank you, Mr. Slaughterback. You've been very helpful," said Agent Jones.

Principal Slaughterback handed him his business card. "If you have any more questions, don't hesitate to call. Other than that one incident Joseph was a model student."

"Thank you," said Agent Jones. "I'll see myself to the entrance."

Thursday morning Zeke received a call at eight am. "This is Special Agent Jones. I'm sure you remember me. I'd like to come by WJOP to talk with you."

"What more trouble could I be in?" asked Zeke. "You already suspended my clearance."

"Well," said Mr. Jones. "It's complicated. How's ten o'clock this morning?"

"That's good," said Zeke. "See you then."

At ten o'clock, Zeke got a call from Julie. "Zeke, Agent Jones is here to see you."

"I'll be right down," said Zeke. He went down to the reception area to find Agent Jones and Abby Sorensen, his assistant, in the conference room. "Hi, Miss Sorensen, good to see you again. So, Mr. Jones, what's going on with my clearance?"

"Excuse me," interrupted Abby. "I just want to let you know that I am recording this interview."

"OK, that's fine with me," replied Zeke.

"I made a visit to your high school," said Agent Jones. "Clearly, you have not been forthcoming with us. The last time we talked you neglected to tell us the whole story."

"Look, what can I do to make it right?" asked Zeke. "I really need this clearance."

"This is a matter of integrity, Zeke," continued Agent Jones. "If we can't trust you, what do you expect?"

"My lawyer told me I'd never have to tell anyone. He said it would be as if it never happened," replied Zeke.

"That's just not the case, Zeke. I advise you to talk to an attorney. This time get a Security Clearance Attorney. I'm recommending that your clearance continue to be suspended pending a review board. I don't know when you're telling the truth. Furthermore, if they find to revoke your clearance permanently, it's possible that the agency may want to prosecute you for fraud."

"No, please don't do that," said Zeke. "I'm not a threat to anyone. I'm just a guy applying for a clearance so that I can do my job."

"Zeke, I'll get back to you with the decision of the review board."

"I guess all I can do is wait," said Zeke.

"That's about it, kid," Agent. Jones replied as he extended his hand to Zeke. Zeke reciprocated with a handshake and direct eye contact, while wondering what he could ask him.

"Aha," said Zeke, "I know what to ask you. Mr. Jones, is the FBI really gonna charge me for lying on my current clearance application?"

"No," answered Mr. Jones. "The FBI has bigger fish to fry. We just want to scare you into telling the truth."

"Will the FBI re-instate my current clearance?" asked Zeke.

Before Agent Jones could answer, Zeke felt a kick to his midsection. The kick sent him back into the conference room wall, and separated him from Agent Jones, breaking his handshake connection.

"Don't say anything more," Zeke heard Abby shout at Agent Jones.

Agent Jones appeared dazed. "What's going on?"

"Don't you know?" responded Abby.

"I was just saying goodbye," replied Harry.

"Zeke has the ability to extract truth from a person," said Abby. "When he grasps your hand and looks you in the eye, he locks on and you will tell the truth to any question he chooses to ask."

"I just thought that was a bunch of nonsense," said Harry.

Zeke heard Abby say, "Let's get out of here before he gets anything else."

As Abby and Harry left the building, Abby pitched an idea to Harry. "So, Harry, what do you think about Zeke's unique ability?"

"I'm glad you stepped in and kicked him back when you did," said Harry.

"Why? What do you mean?"

"He didn't get much with the first question," said Harry.

"So, you were aware of what he was asking?" asked Abby.

"Yes. At first, I was dazed, but I remember clearly now. He asked me if we were really gonna charge him for lying on his clearance, and I told him, no. Then, he asked me if we were going to re-instate his clearance, and you kicked him back."

"So, you concur that his ability is for real?" said Abby.

"Yeah, it's for real," replied Harry.

"Well, Harry, I'm sure you're aware that the Secret Service has contacted us about a possible assassination plot on both the president and vice president."

"Yes, so what's that got to do with Zeke Jackson?" asked Harry.

"I think we could use Zeke to ferret out what's going on," replied Abby. "Zeke has the ability to get a person talking, not just yes or no answers."

"We'll just let the CIA take care of it. They'll waterboard 'em, and then, they'll start talking," said Harry.

"What if we had a way of getting the information without waterboarding? This could be a great plus for the FBI. Besides, we can't waterboard our own senators, congressmen, or congresswomen," said Abby.

"You think our own government is involved in planning an assassination plot on the president and vice president?"

"It would not surprise me," replied Abby.

"OK, look," said Harry. "I'll get an appointment with the FBI director and see what he thinks."

"Thanks, Harry. Can I join you?" asked Abby. "I've watched him every time he's been on TV."

"OK. I've only seen the interview with Fernando Dollar," said Harry. "That's probably a good idea."

Meanwhile, before Zeke went back to his cubicle, he talked with Julie at the reception desk.

"Are you OK, Zeke?" Julie asked. "I saw that kick to the stomach that you took from that Agent Sorensen. What was that all about?"

"I went into my truth mode on Mr. Jones, grasping his hand and asking him some questions. Then, Abby saw what I was doing and tried to stop me. She was just doing her job."

"So, are they going to reinstate your clearance?" asked Julie.

"According to Mr. Jones, they're going to send it to a review board. They're taking a hard line. I asked him if the FBI was going to reinstate my clearance, but that's when Abby kicked me."

After Zeke went upstairs, he passed by Harvey's office.

Harvey called to him, "Zeke, come in here."

"Yeah, Boss, what's up?"

"I hear you met with the FBI investigator again," replied Harvey. "Agent Jones called me before he came over. How did it go?"

"Not too well," replied Zeke. "In fact, they're talking about charging me with fraud because they don't think I've been forthcoming about my past. I've already told you about most of it."

"Well, let's have the rest of it," said Harvey.

Zeke told Harvey about the two teachers and Agent Jones additional recent investigation at his high school.

"I see," said Harvey. "You got off pretty easy, kid. Kids never think that what they do will follow them for the rest of their life."

"Yeah, I can certainly attest to that." Zeke's eyes teared up. "I was responsible for the deaths of two people. Not a day goes by that I don't think about that."

"Look, kid, you've got to move on with the rest of your life. You've got to put it behind you. Thinking about this all the time will tear you up. I think you really ought to talk to headquarters. I told you they're talking about how to give you your own show or put you on some other show on a regular basis. That could be epic for your career. Like I said before, you're talking book deals, speeches, appearances, stuff you can't even imagine at this time in your life. I could help you out. You know I have contacts there. And, all this clearance stuff will be history. Also, you could be a big help to us here at WJOP. It can't hurt to have an inside man at headquarters."

"Not what I ever intended for my career," said Zeke. "But, in light of my current circumstances, it's looking better. Let me think about it."

"Don't take too long," said Harvey. "Now's the best time to jump on this while it's fresh in their minds."

"By the way," said Zeke. "Some of this stuff about my high school, the FBI did not uncover it by themselves. Someone from this station anonymously told them. You wouldn't have any idea who that would be, would ya?"

"Zeke, I have reporters, cameramen, and techs applying for clearances all the time. Many of them are granted access to high-up officials, including the president and vice president, congressmen and women, and senators. The people who work at WJOP are patriots. If they see something concerning national security that they don't think is right, they'll act on it, and I support them. We are very dependent on the FBI for clearances. Whatever we can do to enhance our image with the FBI is good with me. So, no, I don't know who ratted on you, and I wouldn't tell you even if I did. Sorry, Zeke. I can't help you with the clearance."

"Thanks a lot, Boss," said Zeke, as he left Harvey's office. Zeke's smile faded, and his broad shoulders began to droop. Zeke could not understand a boss like this. "It's like he wants me to fail. He definitely does not have my back," he murmured under his breath as he shuffled back to his cubicle.

Zeke was never treated like this when he worked for CBS affiliate, KOLN, in Lincoln, Nebraska. He was doted on. The award-winning newsman, they used to call him.

When he arrived at his cubicle, Zeke called Julie. "Hey, Julie, how about lunch?"

"I was hoping you'd call," said Julie. "Meet me in ten?"

"Sure," replied Zeke.

Zeke met Julie at the front reception desk.

"You're in for a treat today," said Zeke. "I'm taking you to the Copper Canyon Grill in Silver Spring. It's not very far, and a great place, I hear. Plus, I need some cheering up after the day I've had. So, let's treat ourselves."

Zeke and Julie took Zeke's truck and headed down Georgia Avenue to downtown Silver Spring until they got to the restaurant at Georgia Avenue and Colesville Road. They parked and walked a few blocks to the restaurant.

"Football weather," said Zeke. "I love it."

"What?" asked Julie.

"The air's changing; I can feel it. I can smell it. Hail to the Redskins, HTTR," shouted Zeke.

"Wait a minute. Redskins are my team. You can't come here and act like a Skins fan. You have to earn that through years of sorrow and disappointment," said Julie. "Anyway, you can't call them the Redskins anymore. They changed the name. They're the Washington Football Team now."

"So, I've heard," replied Zeke. "Hail to the Washington Football Team, HTTWFT."

"Doesn't sound the same," said Julie. "Now, I know you're not really a Skins fan. A real Skins fan would never call them the Washington Football Team."

"Well, it doesn't really matter. If Harvey has his way, I'll be rooting for the Giants or the Jets."

"What do you mean?" asked Julie.

"He wants me to work at Blackrock Headquarters. He said headquarters was so impressed with my performance on the *Jack Cong* show that they want to make me a regular or even give me my own show. I told Harry I want to report the news, not be the news. I don't like sensationalism."

They entered the restaurant and were seated at one of the side tables. Upbeat, soft jazz mixed with the low light to create a sophisticated atmosphere. Over at a table in the corner of the room sat a group of four young boys, ages three or four, and a mom celebrating a birthday.

"This is not like any restaurant I've ever been to," said Julie. "Elegant yet homey. I can't believe I've lived in this area for several years and have never been here. This restaurant is so you: a little bit country, a little bit jazz, but all American."

"Wait until you taste the food," said Zeke. The waiter approached, and Zeke asked for a drink menu.

After looking through it, Julie said with a grin, "I'll have a Manhattan, stirred, not shaken."

"Who would dare to shake a Manhattan?" replied the waiter.

"Really," said Zeke. "I'll have one, too."

"I'll be back with your drinks. Meanwhile, do you have any questions about the menu?" asked the waiter.

"No," replied Zeke.

"Manhattans are an acquired taste," said Julie, "much like the city after which they are named."

"Are you trying to tell me something?" asked Zeke.

"Maybe," said Julie. "You shouldn't be afraid to try new things."

"What are you talking about?" asked Zeke. "I moved from Nebraska to DC, remember?"

"But you're still thinking like a Cornhusker," said Julie.

"What do you mean?" asked Zeke.

"I hate to be the one to tell you this," said Julie. "But you're still a bit of a country bumpkin. Always waiting for everything to make sense, to turn out in your preconceived notion of the way things ought to be."

The waiter returned with two Manhattans, each garnished with an orange twist and a maraschino cherry.

"Have you decided on your entrée?" asked the waiter.

"I'll have the rotisserie chicken with mashed potatoes," said Julie.

"I'll have the prime rib medium with mashed potatoes," said Zeke.

"Excellent choices," replied the waiter. "It'll be ready in about twenty minutes. Enjoy your Manhattans."

"You know, Zeke. I would love to live in New York," said Julie. "All those shows, the night life, the clubs. DC is so droll. Government and politicians. Everybody running around in suits trying to impress one another. Lawyers running around like leeches on the backs of people's lives trying to maintain their respectable images. I'm not going anywhere in this town. I can get a receptionist job anywhere, maybe even at BlackRock. Zeke, you should really consider it. The possibility of having your own show or even being a regular on a network show, that's unbelievable. I could be watching you on New Year's Eve hosting the dropping of the ball."

"You're starting to sound like Harvey," replied Zeke.

"It's lightning," said Julie. "It's a career lightning strike, and it's striking you. What's the worst that could happen? If it doesn't work out, you could always go home to Nebraska. Forget the news reporting and the clearance thing. Go for the brass ring."

The waiter arrived with the food.

"The chicken rotisserie looks like a work of art. I don't know whether to eat it or just look at it," said Julie. Julie pulled her phone from her purse and took a picture of both entrées.

"You two have just ordered our two most favorite entrées," said the waiter. "Bon appétit."

Zeke devoured his steak with gusto. "Arguably, the best prime rib in the DC area," said Zeke.

"The chicken is so juicy," said Julie, "but I can't finish it all."

The waiter returned and asked if they wanted dessert. "Our bread pudding comes highly recommended," said the waiter.

"Not this time," said Zeke. "Just the check, please and a box for the chicken. Everything was great."

"This has been a great lunch," said Julie. "I needed a treat today. Thanks, Zeke. We'll have to come here again."

"Thank you," replied Zeke. "This conversation has clarified some things for me. You've given me some things to think about."

The waiter returned with the check and box for Julie's chicken. After exiting the restaurant, they returned to Zeke's car. As Zeke opened the door for Julie, she slipped her hand between his left arm and torso, pulled him close, stood on her toes, and kissed him on the cheek.

"I'm gonna miss that in New York," said Zeke.

Julie made a pouty face at Zeke but said nothing. On the drive back to the station, Julie blurted out, "You know, I think I'm going to break it off with Harvey."

Zeke looked at her shocked. "Whoa, where did that come from?"

"Come on," she said. "Don't act like you didn't know."

"I've haven't been here that long," said Zeke. "I'm not up on all the office affairs and politics."

"Well, it's true. I've been seeing him, but he's married and twice my age," said Julie.

Zeke was careful not to violate Harvey's trust, but he could not help but show a slight smile. "Don't do this on my account," he said.

"You don't fool me. I see that smile," said Julie. "Don't flatter yourself. We hardly know each other, but he's a dead-end street. That relationship is going nowhere."

"Well, I'd agree with that," said Zeke.

When they arrived back at the station, Julie returned to the reception desk and Zeke returned upstairs to find Harvey by his cubicle.

"Long lunch, kid?" asked Harvey. "Look, while you're still working here, there's a story I want you to work on. You can do it all with phone calls and some googling. Maybe some archive research. So, you won't need any special access or clearance."

"What is it?" asked Zeke.

"There are some rumors going around that there's an assassination plot brewing against the president and vice president."

"Wow, that's huge," said Zeke.

"Yeah," said Harvey, "but it's totally unsubstantiated. Could be a total hoax. I need you to dig around and find some basis for it. Any facts or even suspicions that have some basis in reality. If we can't do a news story on it, maybe we can turn it into an op-ed. I need you to dig hard, kid. That's what I hired you for."

Zeke thought it over for a few hours while scouring the Web to see if there was any talk of an assassination plot. He found nothing. He figured that if there was such a plot, the Secret Service, the FBI, and CIA would be in the know, but they probably wouldn't give him squat. So, he decided to call one of the only two contacts he had at the FBI, Abby Sorensen.

"Miss Sorensen, this is Zeke Jackson."

"Hi, Zeke," said Abby. "Are you calling about your clearance?"

"No, I'm calling to tell you that your kick didn't break any bones."

"Well, my mistake," said Abby. "I must not have landed it correctly. I'll have to work on that."

"Ha, ha," replied Zeke. "Actually, this is a business call. I'm working on a story about a possible assassination plot on the president and vice president. The Web is totally quiet on this, but here at the station, we've heard some rumors."

"I can't talk about that," said Abby.

"Oh, so you acknowledge there is some such plot?" asked Zeke.

"I acknowledge no such thing," said Abby.

"Can I meet you for lunch tomorrow?" asked Zeke.

"What?" Abby asked surprised.

"Can I meet you for lunch tomorrow? You know, that thing you do in the middle of the day when you get hungry?" asked Zeke.

"I don't know…," replied Abby. "I guess."

"OK," said Zeke. "I'll meet you at Harriet's Family Restaurant at noon. It's only a block from the FBI headquarters.

"Yeah, I know where it is," said Abby. "See you tomorrow."

Zeke pondered whether he should let Harvey know. He decided not to, feeling Harvey had been more interested in getting rid of him than anything else. Instead, Zeke went home for the day.

The next day, as Zeke arrived at the station and walked up the long set of white stone steps, for the first time he encountered the ducks from the pond about fifty yards away. They were pooping all over the pristine white stone, staining and tarnishing its stately and respectable image. As he approached the arched entrance, he heard the sounds of truck engines coming from the back of the station as they round the driveway to the front of the building.

"Zeke, jump in here," yelled Sly. Zeke ran over to Sly's truck.

"What's going on?" he asked.

"They're staging a mock trial of the president," Sly replied.

"Who?" asked Zeke.

"The demonstrators. They're outside the barred gates of the White House staging a mock trial," said Sly. "Harvey wants us over there right away. He heard some rumors yesterday about an assassination plot on the president and vice president."

"Yeah, he asked me to look into it."

"Me too," said Sly.

"Figures," replied Zeke.

"Hey, you ought to know Harvey by now," said Sly. "Whatever works is his motto."

The camera trucks moved through traffic like a fire truck on its way to a three-story blaze. On the way they picked up a police escort which gave them right-of-way after they noticed the call letters, WJOP news. After the camera truck arrived at 1600 Pennsylvania Avenue, cameramen jumped from the truck, unpacked their equipment, and setup for live broadcast.

"For high crimes and misdemeanors," shouted the lead demonstrator. "We indict and try this president and his coconspirator, the vice president of the United States. They have torn babies away from their mothers on our southern border and around the United States. They have committed war crimes waterboarding freedom fighters at Guantanamo. They have used their ICE Agency to commit inhumane crimes against undocumented aliens just looking for a better place to live their lives. They have polluted our air and endangered our citizenry with these irresponsible deregulation policies. They have taken from the poor and given to the rich with these unfair tax policies. They are racists and bigots who side with the KKK and the white supremacists who strive to hold down minorities and retain power."

Then, the demonstrators took two fake doll caricatures of the president and vice president and set them on fire. At this point the Capitol Police and the metropolitan police moved in to break up the demonstration while the demonstrators spit in their faces and chanted derogatory remarks prompting some arrests.

Zeke went up to one of the demonstrators with the WJOP camera crew. "Sir, I heard your rhetoric. Do you really think the president and vice president are guilty of all this?" asked Zeke.

"Where have you been, man? Can't you see it?"

"Why don't you just organize and vote them out?" asked Zeke.

"We're trying, and we intend to," said the demonstrator. "We'll get rid of them one way or another."

"What do you mean?" asked Zeke.

"You figure it out, man. Their days are numbered. I'd like to turn them over to the freedom fighters they call terrorists and let them administer real justice."

"And that's the scene here in front of the White House this chilly, sunny morning in September. Now, back to, Jamie Ryan, our newscaster back at the station."

"Thanks, Zeke. The demonstrators are not happy campers," said Jamie. "WJOP is following this story and will keep you updated."

"Sly," called Zeke. "I've got to talk to an agent from the FBI, so I won't be riding back with you."

"Clearance problems, again?" asked Sly.

"No, but what would you know about it?" replied Zeke."

"Oh, nothing. Overheard others talking. Good luck."

Zeke hailed a cab to Harriet's Family Restaurant.

"Hey, man, were you just at the demonstration?" asked the cabbie.

"Yeah," said Zeke. "I work for WJOP."

"I've been driving a cab in this city for the last forty years," said the cabbie. "Back then they were rioting against Nixon. It never changes. Just a different decade."

"I wouldn't know," said Zeke. "I'm only twenty-five and just came here in August."

"Hey, I know you," blurted the cabbie. "You're that truth guy. I saw you take down Fernando Dollar. Then, I saw that interview with Jack Cong. Wait till I tell my wife. She won't believe it. Well, here's the restaurant." Zeke handed the cabbie a twenty-dollar bill."

"Good luck, truth man," said the cabbie. "I'll look for you on TV again."

Zeke walked into the seemingly unimpressive restaurant.

"How many?" asked the greeter.

"Two," said Zeke. The greeter led Zeke to a table in the center of the room where Abby could easily spot him when she entered the restaurant. He ordered a cup of coffee and pondered the questions he was going to ask her. He figured he'd lead with the demonstration that just happened. He'd tell her what the demonstrator said. To Zeke, it sounded like the kind of talk that would at least prompt some investigation, at least by the Secret Service. After all, their main objective is security of the president and vice president. Abby finally walked in and the greeter ushered her over to Zeke's table.

"Hi, Abby. Thanks for coming."

"Can we switch tables?" asked Abby. "Someplace a little more inconspicuous. A lot of people I work with come here for lunch, and I don't want a lot of questions when I get back to the office."

"Sure," said the greeter. "Follow me." The greeter led them to a table in another room. "How's this?" she asked.

"This is fine," said Abby.

"How did you come to work for the FBI?" asked Zeke.

"Well, I majored in criminology at University of Maryland in College Park with a minor in computer science. But I applied for the CIA directly out of college. They sent recruiters over to the university. They liked me, and I applied. It was a long, drawn-out application process. Eventually, I was rejected."

"Why was that? "asked Zeke.

"I passed all their security stuff, but then they gave me a psychological test to see if I was a good fit. They decided I was not. I didn't have enough analytical or technical background to use me as an analyst, and I wasn't suited to their kind of field agent work. So, I went to work for the FBI. By the way, that's what I want to talk to you about."

"What? Going to work for the FBI?" asked Zeke facetiously.

"Yeah, right," said Abby sarcastically.

The waiter arrived and asked for their drink order.

"I'll have unsweetened ice tea," said Abby.

"Same for me," said Zeke.

"We're ready to order our entrées," said Abby. "I'll have the salmon Caesar salad."

"Sounds good," said Zeke. "I'll have that, too."

"Well, Zeke, what is it you wanted to talk to me about?"

"I just got back from covering a demonstration that was happening in front of the White House," replied Zeke.

"I know," said Abby. "We were watching it live at the office. I was wondering if you were going to make it here on time."

"Actually, I'm supposed to be writing a story on a possible presidential and vice-presidential assassination plot. Then, this morning I got called to hop on a camera truck to this demonstration. I wonder if this demonstration was the smoke before the fire."

"Well, Zeke, I can't really say. I can't be a source for you, but I can tell you that you're onto something. Keep pursuing it. Not to change the subject, but do you still want your clearance back?"

"Are you kidding?" asked Zeke. "You know I do."

"Well, this is a roundabout way of getting it, but I have an idea. Your clearance currently remains suspended. The FBI can indefinitely suspend it, in which case, who knows if you'll ever get it back. You need a fresh start. My partner, Harry, has gone to bat for you, but the agency is just not sure about you. They know you were underage and that your record was expunged, but they are reluctant to take a chance on someone who committed such an egregious act even if it was a prank by a fourteen-year-old."

"So, what do you have in mind?" asked Zeke.

"I suggest that you see a security clearance attorney. Here's the number for Jackmann's Law Firm. They specialize in clearances. Maybe they can file something to allow you to re-apply, but this time through a different agency, one more friendly to your situation. I have some contacts in the CIA from the exhausting interviewing process I went through. I think they would be very interested in your special gift."

"Do you think they would overlook my bomb scare incident?" asked Zeke.

"Yes, I do, if you are totally forthcoming about it. You'd need to gain their confidence. Let me make some calls and establish their interest level. Then, if they're definitely interested, I'll find out the process they want you to follow."

"Would they restore my press pass and let me in the White House for press briefings?" asked Zeke.

"I can't think of why they wouldn't," replied Abby.

"Say the CIA decided to bring me on in some capacity. Could I still work as a reporter at WJOP and cover White House stuff?"

"I told my partner, Harry, that you were no country bumpkin, but you still got a little bit of it left. Zeke, if you get through the CIA process, you won't need a press pass anymore. You'll be the CIA's man to the Secret Service. But, if you want to join the press in the East Room, I'm sure they won't mind," said Abby.

"Wow, thanks," said Zeke. "But why are you doing all this for me?"

"Well, I interview a lot of people for clearances. I think you deserve a second chance. So, keep this on the down low at work. Plus, I believe the CIA, the Secret Service, and yes, the FBI could all make good use of your special gift. Not to mention, I think you're a good guy."

"I don't know what to say," said Zeke. "It's not like anybody has been stroking my ego lately. So, thanks for the vote of confidence."

Zeke and Abby finished their lunch and left the restaurant. Zeke took a cab back to the station. On the way, he called Jackmann's Law Firm and made an appointment to see one of the clearance attorneys.

When Zeke entered the reception area, Julie stopped him.

"Where have you been?" Julie asked.

"Well, as I was coming into the station, literally climbing the steps, Sly snagged me to go with him to a demonstration in front of the White House. Then I had an interview with an FBI investigator," replied Zeke.

"Which one?" asked Julie.

"Abby Sorensen," replied Zeke.

"I thought so," said Julie. "I think she's got a thing for you."

"No, she just wants to help me," said Zeke.

"What do you mean, she just wants to help you?"

"It's nothing," said Zeke with a look of irritation."

Zeke felt his cell phone vibrating. "Hey, Boss," answered Zeke.

"Zeke, can you stop by my office?"

"Sure thing, Boss."

Zeke walked up stairs to the second floor and stopped by the break room for a cup coffee. He met Ellie from the social media news desk.

"Hey, Zeke," said Ellie. "That interview you did this morning is trending on social media. Did you know that headquarters is tracking every time you're on the air? They're tracking all the social media activity from your broadcasts or appearances. They're monitoring the buzz you create. I get calls from the BlackRock CBS news department every day wanting stats on you. I think you're their new golden child. I'm surprised Harvey hasn't told you about it. He's been aware of it for some time now."

"Speaking of Harvey, I think he wants to see me. Thanks for the info, Ellie. Please let me know if you see or hear of anything interesting concerning me."

"Sure thing," replied Ellie. "I'll keep you posted."

Zeke reported to Harvey's office. He found Julie there.

"Come in, Zeke. I was just asking Julie to set up a luncheon for the office. I think it's time we celebrate. Our ratings last month were off the charts. Julie, we can talk about this later. I've got some things that I need to discuss with Zeke."

Julie brushed her hand against Zeke's arm as she left the room.

"Do you have anything yet on that assassination plot? The demonstration this morning could be an indicator of something more sinister in the works."

"I did some searching on social media but didn't pull up anything," replied Zeke.

"Listen, kid, I don't pay you to find stuff on social media and then write a story about it. I pay you to dig up stuff, and write a story that social media then picks up and runs with. What am I running here, a daycare for news reporters? Now, what do ya got?"

"I got nothin'. Nothin' at all," said Zeke. "Without these clearances, I have access to no one."

"Well, kid. You better start thinking real serious about BlackRock. They're calling here every day asking about your availability. Maybe I was wrong about you. Maybe you're not cut out to be a newsman. Maybe, a talk show host like Jack Cong, is your thing."

For a minute Zeke said nothing. Then, he took a deep breath, looked Harvey in the eye and said, "Don't worry Boss. I'll figure out something."

He refrained from saying anything more and turned and walked away. The ability to not be goaded into an argument was something he learned from his father. His mind wandered back to Nebraska and the people there. Life was so much kinder, even when he messed up. It was hunting season there. He thought about going home for a couple of days. Then, he remembered the appointment had with a clearance attorney that evening.

At 6:00 pm, Zeke drove to downtown DC to Jackmann's Law Firm.

"Hello, Zeke. I'm Attorney Daniel Bogsley. I understand you're having a problem with your current clearance."

"That's right. My clearance was recently suspended after they discovered a crime for which I was convicted as a minor," said Zeke. From there, Zeke proceeded to fill him in on all the specifics of his case.

"Well," said the attorney. "If I had a hundred dollars for every young man whose attorney told them, 'Your records will be expunged. It'll be just like it never happened,' I could've retired by now. You're probably facing a suspension and possible revoke based on Guideline E, Personal Conduct, for alleged intentional omission. I'll file a response to the Statement of Reasons (SOR) that the government gives for a clearance revoke. I'll tell them that you were advised by your attorney not to list the incident. I'll also tell them that you want to apply to another agency and that you'll correct and re-submit your SF-86. I think this will take care of it."

"Thank you! Thank you! Thank you!" exclaimed Zeke.

"That's what I'm here for. I do this all the time. Hey, in DC, a clearance is a must. You got a clearance, you got a job. That's why we're in business."

6

A Walk in the Park

The next day, Zeke woke up and called Harvey to tell him that his aunt had died, and that he needed to go home for a few days. Harvey told him to take all the time he needed and that he would turn the story over to Sly. Zeke called home and talked to his dad, and told him that he was coming home for a few days to sort things out. His parents told him they would pick him up at Lincoln Airport. Zeke called Julie to let her know that he was going home for a few days. He also told her that his aunt had died.

Zeke decided to take the next plane back to Lincoln, Nebraska, from Reagan National Airport. As he made his way through the airport, he became aware of people staring at him again.

One gentleman in particular seemed to be fixated on him. Finally, the man, dressed in a suit, approached Zeke and asked him, "Aren't you that guy who interviewed Fernando Dollar?"

Zeke had become tired of people asking this, but he played along. "Yes, that was me."

"Well, it's a pleasure to meet you," said the man. "I'm U.S. Congressman Jack Johnson, Chairman of the Intelligence Committee."

Zeke was not overly surprised. Reagan National Airport was well known for flying many of the nation's congressmen and senators.

"Well, nice to meet you, Congressman."

"Son, you have quite a gift."

"That's what people keep telling me, but it's nothing I had anything to do with," replied Zeke.

"Nonetheless," said the congressman. "Perhaps it was given to you for the good of others. Something to think about."

"Thanks. I'll give it some thought," said Zeke.

The two departed, and Zeke boarded his plane. In two and a half hours, he would be back in Nebraska, away from the DC and East Coast insanity. Hopefully, he could think more clearly.

Zeke's mom and dad were waiting for him in the cell lot when he arrived at Lincoln Airport. As he deboarded the plane, he called them and they drove to the pickup zone.

When Zeke walked out of the terminal to the pickup zone, his parents shouted, "Joseph, Joseph, over here."

He went to their car and his mom, Joan, jumped out and immediately embraced him.

"It's been so long, Joseph." They hadn't seen him since he left in August. It was almost October.

"Hi, son," said his father. "Welcome home. Now, we need to go. We're backing up traffic."

Zeke laughed. "This ain't traffic."

"I'll have you know that Lancaster County is now the second most populated county in Nebraska," said his dad.

"Yeah, but it's still Nebraska," replied Zeke.

"What's wrong with Nebraska?" asked his dad. "Lincoln is hardly some backwoods, unsophisticated place."

"Yeah, I know, Dad. You would not believe what I've been through the last couple of months," said Zeke.

"We've been following you as best we could. We saw the Fernando Dollar interview and the Jack Cong interview."

"Wouldn't hurt if you called home more often," said his mom.

"I expected the fast pace. I expected the traffic. I expected sweltering heat. I even expected the hardness of people," said Zeke. "But I did not expect how cruel people can be. Did I tell you that someone from my office reported me on the FBI's whistleblower line and told them about the bomb scare?"

"How could they have found that out?" asked his dad.

"It was my coworker. We went out after work. I had a couple drinks. He noticed my real name on a book at the office and began asking me questions. I thought I didn't tell him much, but it must've been enough to cause the FBI to suspend my clearance and re-investigate me. They found out that two teachers died the day of the bomb scare."

"Son, you've got to be more careful not to spread that around. That's all been dealt with. That's all in the past. Your records were expunged. I know how bad you feel about Mr. Clayborn and Mr. Jenkins dying that day but, truth be told, it really was their three hundred pounds and smoking that killed them."

"I still feel terrible about it," replied Zeke.

"You know, I ran into Rita Sykes, the high school secretary, at the grocery store. She told me that someone had come to the school asking questions about Joseph, specifically about the bomb scare."

"Well, never mind that for now," said Zeke. "I've got bigger things to think about."

"Let's just get you home, son, and you can tell us all about it. We can sort through this thing together. Hey, Joseph, later maybe we could go over to Wilderness Park," said his dad. "You always loved that park."

"Yeah," said Zeke. "I made the biggest decisions of my life while walking through that park."

"I think it's time for another walk," said his dad. "This time I'd like to tag along if it's all right with you."

"Sounds good to me," replied Zeke.

As Zeke and his parents pulled into the driveway, their golden Lab appeared in the living room window barking.

"Cucho," Zeke yelled. "Boy, have I missed you."

Zeke jumped from the car and ran to the door. He quickly unlocked it and opened the door. Cucho darted out the door to jump on Zeke knocking him back into the yard. Zeke fell backward with Cucho on top, and there they renewed an old friendship. When they finished playing, they went into the modest brick house in which Zeke had spent his entire life before the military and college and to which he always returned.

"We have a surprise for you," teased his mom. Aunt Becky came walking out of the kitchen.

"Joseph," she cried with soggy eyes, and they embraced one another.

"It's like a homecoming," Zeke exclaimed.

"Exactly," said Aunt Becky. "Your mom told me that you were coming home this morning. There was no way I was not going to be here. I even cancelled my hairdresser appointment, and that woman is not easy to get."

"Let's have lunch," said Zeke's mom. "Becky, would you help me put the lunchmeat and fixings out on the dining room table?"

"Sure," Becky replied.

"By the way, Aunt Becky, you're dead," said Zeke. "That's what I told my boss so I could get away for a few days."

"Well, it's not the first time I died. I remember when your father did the same thing to get a few days off."

"Wonderful thing, that bereavement leave," said his dad. "Everybody needs a break once in a while, and there's no arguing with bereavement leave."

Zeke and his dad went into the dining room and sat down. "Now, don't you two start the conversation without us," said Aunt Becky.

"Wouldn't think of it, you old busy body," said Zeke's dad, Rodger. After Zeke's mom, Joan, and Aunt Becky set the table and brought in all the food, Rodger began the conversation.

"So, Joseph, we all saw the two interviews. By the way, I have some things I want to ask you about all that, but it can wait. Tell us what we don't know," said Rodger.

Zeke recapped his trip to CBS headquarters for his parents. "CBS headquarters contacted my boss and told him they wanted to find a place for me at headquarters as a regular on the *Jack Cong* show or my own show."

"Joseph, that is an absolute miracle," said his mom.

"Not so fast, Joan," said his dad. "Let's hear the rest of it."

"Meanwhile, I had a couple of visits from the FBI concerning my clearance," continues Zeke. "A whistleblower from the station phoned in some info about me claiming I defrauded them on my clearance application. So, they suspended my clearance. This is a real problem because I need it to work as a news reporter in DC. Without it, I might as well get out of the news business. My boss wants me to go to work at headquarters. So, he's pushing me out."

"Because you lost the clearance?" asked his mom.

"That's part of it, I guess," said Zeke. "But, it's more than that. He thinks it'll be good for him to have someone at headquarters. It gives the station some connections, and he's always wanted to work there. Just before I left for home, my boss asked me to look into a story about a potential assassination plot on the president and vice president."

"Oh, my God," exclaimed his mom. "Is it true?"

"I don't know, Mom," replied Zeke. "But, I'm gonna try to find out."

"Well, how are you going to do that?" asked his mom.

"I don't know. If I had a clearance, I think it would be easier. Abby Sorensen, Agent Jones's assistant, offered to help me get my clearance back."

Zeke told his mom, dad and Aunt Becky about the interview with the Agent Jones and Agent Sorensen.

"Why does she want to help you, son?" asked his Dad.

"She said she thinks I got a bad deal and that I'm actually a good guy."

"Rodger, you are so dense. You too, for that matter, Joseph," said his mom.

"What do you mean?" asked Zeke.

"She likes you. That's why she's helping you. It's just that simple."

"Yeah, but in the interview, she kicked me to get me away from her boss."

"What?" asked his mom.

"I was shaking Agent Jones's hand. She kicked me to stop me from asking him questions."

"It was a love tap," said his mom. "Look, you guys think a woman has got to be showering you with physical attention to show their interest. Good girls just start doing things for you."

"Anyway, Joseph, if you could use your gift to get information out of Agent Jones, you could use it to interrogate those demonstrators you were telling us about," said his mom.

"So, son, when do you actually know the answer to the questions that you're asking a person?" asked his father.

"I know the answer as soon as I ask it," said Zeke. "As long as I have a grip on their hand and am making eye contact."

"So, you don't actually have to ask the question?" asked his dad.

"That's right. I see their spiritual condition and I know their answer before they say it."

"Becky, you're awfully quiet," said Rodger her brother. "What do you think about this gift?"

"I'm just taking it all in," answered Aunt Becky. "It sounds like the gift of knowledge to me. I think we should all lay hands on Joseph and pray for him. I don't know what's going on here, but I know a God thing when I see it."

Rodger chimed in, "We may not all agree on church matters, but long ago I promised the Lord that I would raise my family up in the Lord. Let's all gather around Joseph and pray for him."

Rodger, Joan, and Aunt Becky stood up around Zeke's chair, laid a hand on him, and then prayed for his protection and that God would use him in the best way He saw fit in accordance with His Almighty, divine will.

"Mom, Dad, Aunt Becky," said Zeke. "I want to thank you all for your love, prayers, and support. I don't know how all this is going to turn out, but it's comforting to know that I have a family like this."

"Now, Joseph, I have a little surprise for you," said his dad. "Let's you and I take a drive to Wilderness Park where we can go for a good walk and reacquaint with God's nature, something you probably don't see much in DC."

"Yeah, I'd like that," said Zeke. "Can we bring Cucho?"

"Of course," said his dad.

"Have some good bonding time," said his mom.

Zeke got Cucho, and they jumped in the car and drove for about five miles southwest to Lincoln's largest park, Wilderness Park. The park was considered a city park, but compared to DC, it was pure wilderness, thirteen miles of horse trails and bison. The only time Washingtonians and New Yorkers saw bison was when it was a lean burger on a menu in a restaurant.

After they arrived at the park, they were greeted by two men that Zeke knew from growing up in Lincoln, Pastor Williams from the Pentecostal Apostolic Church in Lincoln and Pastor Jones from the Southern Temple Baptist Church in Lincoln. There were not two men who disagreed more on matters concerning faith and the Christian religion.

Before they got out of the car, Zeke looked at his dad and said, "Pastor Jones and Pastor Williams. Why are they here?"

They got out of the car, and Zeke's dad said, "Joseph, you know these two gentlemen."

"Yes," said Zeke. "Pastor Jones, Pastor Williams. It's been a while. Good to see you both, but I would not expect to see you two in the same place."

"Well," said Pastor Williams, "I know this comes as a surprise, but your dad called and asked us to be here today to help with some decisions you are making. He's filled us in on a lot of what's been going on in your life lately and thought we might be able to bring clarity. He knows how different our views are on certain matters, and he wanted to have both views represented."

"Well, let's get started on a trail," said Zeke's dad. "We can walk and talk."

The trails in Wilderness Park were not paved. They were dirt trails with potholes, sticks, leaves, and remnants of small trees sometimes strewn across. Close attention needed to be paid when walking these trails. Even closer attention when jogging. Zeke was concerned that the more elderly Pastor Jones would have difficulty traversing a trail.

Thinking the Homestead Trail might be their safest bet, Zeke suggested they take that.

"You mean the thirteen-mile trail?" asked Pastor Jones.

"Think you're up to it, Pastor?" asked Zeke.

"I think I can manage."

"OK. Come on, Cucho," said Zeke.

They started out on the trail. It was fall and the leaves were starting to change color.

"Beautiful," said Pastor Jones.

"Best time of year," said Zeke, as they walked along the narrow, unpaved road. "The day I decided to join the Marines I came out here to walk and pray about my decision. Then, when I got out of the Marines, I came out here again and spent the day walking and talking to God."

"What happened, Joseph?" asked Pastor Williams.

"What do you mean?" asked Zeke.

"You were totally on fire for the Lord in high school," said Pastor Williams. "After college, I never saw you again. What happened?"

"I guess I lost my faith," replied Zeke.

"Son, you don't just lose your faith, unless you never had it to begin with," said Pastor Jones.

"Oh, he had it," retorted Pastor Williams. "That boy was so excited. He was on fire for the Lord. After I baptized him in the Spirit, he started praying in tongues. He started prophesying."

"Ron," said Pastor Jones, "that don't mean he was saved. Just because someone starts blabbering like a fool don't mean he's saved."

"Listen, Harley, you old coot, we've got a dozen Holiness churches in Lincoln right now and more coming. Southern Baptist are down to four and losing more people by the week. Now, why do you think that is?"

"I don't know, Ron. Maybe, it's 'cause you're teachin' a false gospel that they like to hear. Maybe, it's 'cause your hyping 'em all up on sugar water by feeding 'em all that spirit stuff, convincing 'em that they're gonna get healed of this or that, that God wants 'em to be rich, that they're not gonna have to go through hard times. Hard times is what faith is for. The faith of the true believer grows in times of trouble. Do you want to know what happened to Joseph? I'll tell you what happened. Same thing that's happens to most of our students. Seen it a dozen times. After he got out of the Marines and went off to that university, they argued with him about God. Told him he could never be sure there was a God. Told him that there could be many gods and there are many ways to heaven. Told him the Bible is just a book of literature written by men. Told him Jesus Christ was just a good man like Mohammed. Joseph, did I get it about right?" asked Pastor Jones.

"Yes, Pastor, you nailed it. By the time I graduated college," said Zeke, "I was disillusioned about God and about the meaning and purpose of my life. I stopped going to church. I stopped reading the Bible. I stopped praying."

"Well, enough arguments from you two," said Zeke's dad. "Right now, Zeke needs you to help him determine the legitimacy of this special gift he has. Is it from God? Should he continue to use it? Is it one of the gifts that the Holy Spirit gives? You've both seen his TV interviews."

"Joseph," said Pastor Williams, "can you demonstrate it right now?"

"Yes, I think so," said Zeke.

"Well, demonstrate it on me," said Pastor Williams.

"OK," said Zeke. "Give me your hand and look me in the eye."

Pastor Williams grabbed Zeke's hand and looked him in the eye.

Zeke blurted out, "Your breastplate is damaged."

"What?" asked Pastor Williams.

"Your breastplate is damaged."

"He's talking about the breastplate of righteousness found in the book of Ephesians," said Pastor Jones.

"It has a crack in it," said Zeke. "You have an unclean spirit assaulting you."

"Joseph," said Pastor Jones, "ask him what unholy or unclean thing he's got going on in his life."

"Pastor Williams, are you involved in an unholy activity?" asked Zeke.

"Yes," said Pastor Williams.

"Pastor, what is it?"

"Porn," replied Pastor Williams. "I'm addicted to porn."

"How long?" asked Zeke.

"About two years," replied Pastor Williams. Zeke pulled his hand away.

Pastor Williams, somewhat dazed, looked at Zeke, Pastor Jones, and Rodger and asked, "What's wrong?"

"Do you know what you just admitted to?" asked Zeke.

"I'm not sure. Tell me."

"You just admitted to being addicted to porn," said Zeke.

"Oh no. This will ruin my ministry," Pastor Williams said in fear and remorse as he realized the full extent of his sin.

"Ron," said Pastor Jones, "Let me pray with you." When the two finished praying, Pastor Jones told Pastor Williams, "This doesn't have to become public if you agree to get some help. I think you should tell your elders about this, but that's it. I would be glad to go with you to your next elder's meeting and share our experience and the bad news."

"But," said Pastor Williams, "can't I just get some counseling and leave it at that?"

"Ron," replied Pastor Jones. "Porn addiction is not something that anyone should have, non-Christian or Christian alike. But, a man of the cloth is held to a different standard. I think we should at least tell the elders."

Pastor Jones, Zeke, and his dad laid their hands on Pastor Williams and prayed for him and his deliverance from the addiction and his restoration.

Zeke's dad spoke up. "Actually, the reason I asked you guys to come here today was to help us discern the validity of Joseph's gift. Is it from the Lord? Should he be exercising it? You've both been through seminary and in the ministry for several years. What do you guys think?"

"Well," said Pastor Williams, "gifts of this nature are a continuous debate in Christian circles. But the Pentecostal denominations believe that these gifts are relevant today. The question for me is whether it is from a demonic spirit or the Holy Spirit. It's clear to me that after this experience, this is from the Holy Spirit. It is in keeping with the way the Holy Spirit works."

"I know we don't typically agree, but I would tend to agree with my brother in this instance," said Pastor Jones. "This gift seems to be both discerning and prophetic in nature. It could be the gift of knowledge. It's the degree to which the gift is discerning that intrigues me. The ability to see into another's inner spiritual condition is supernatural and alarming, to say the least, as I'm sure Ron has just experienced. Why God has given this ability to Joseph, I don't know. I can only surmise that He plans to use this gift for something."

"Men," said Pastor Jones, "let's lay hands on Joseph and pray over him that God would use this gift to accomplish His purposes and that Joseph would be a good steward of the gift that the Lord has given him."

After the men finished praying over Zeke, they returned to their cars. They said their goodbyes and drove off. The ride home was very quiet.

Finally, Zeke spoke, "Thanks, Dad. That's exactly what I needed. I feel like I've just been commissioned."

"My pleasure, son, and, yes, you have."

Zeke felt as if he had just come out of a meeting with the Oracle. Only he could understand the full extent of his commissioning, and even now, he did not understand it. But, in time, he would come to know it.

When they got home, Aunt Becky was the first to speak up. "Joseph, how did it go? Are you any clearer now on your purpose?"

"Yes," said Zeke. "Things are making more sense to me now."

Aunt Becky picked up her Bible and turned to the Book of Esther in the Old Testament.

"I think this book has a message for you," said Aunt Becky. "Just as Esther had been made queen and placed in King Ahasuerus's palace for such a time as this. I believe you have been given this divine gift 'for such a time as this.'"

"Thanks, Aunt Becky," said Zeke. "I'll read Esther."

"That's good, sweetheart," said his mom. "And ask that FBI girl out. I like her."

"I get the impression that you've all been collaborating about this all week," replied Zeke.

"We're not as old and senile as you might think," said Aunt Becky. "I got together with your mom and dad, filled them in on what I knew, and then we brainstormed on how we could help. When you decided to come home for a visit, we were ready."

"I'm impressed and thankful," said Zeke. Zeke's cell phone vibrated. It was Abby. "Speak of the devil. It's the FBI girl." Zeke answered.

"Hi, Zeke," greeted Abby. "I've got good news. They want to see you."

"The CIA?" asked Zeke.

"Shhh," replied Abby. "You're gonna need to start keeping this really quiet. When you refer to them, don't say their name. Just call them 'the Agency.' That's how I will refer to them from now on when talking to you. When talking about the FBI, I will always say, the FBI so as not confuse you."

"OK," said Zeke.

"So, the Agency wants to see you tomorrow afternoon at one pm. Can you get back here in time?"

"Oh, I'm back in Nebraska visiting my folks, but I think I can go back to DC now. So, yes I can make it."

"Go to the main headquarters in Langley. I'll text you the address. Ask for Agent Johnson."

"OK," said Zeke. "Will you be there?"

"No," said Abby, "but I'll call you afterward."

"Thanks, Abby. Talk to you soon," said Zeke.

"Folks, I've got to get back to DC. I'm going to try to get a red-eye back to National."

"So soon?" asked his mom. "I'm really starting to dislike this new place you're working.

"Mom, it's my job. I've got to get back. Anyway, I'll be home for Christmas."

"Don't worry, son. Your mom will be OK. Now, let's just have dinner, a relaxing evening, and I'll take you to the airport in the morning," said Zeke's dad.

"Sounds good to me," said Zeke as he wrestled with Cucho.

Zeke made arrangements for a 7:00 am flight from Lincoln Airport to Reagan National. After another home-cooked meal and a relaxing evening, Zeke said goodbye to his mom and Aunt Becky and the family retired for the night. Aunt Becky stayed the night.

The alarm went off at 5:00 am. Zeke and his dad drove to the airport with frost on the car and ground. He wouldn't see that for another month in DC. The two said their goodbyes at the airport. Zeke left home feeling as if it didn't matter what happened in DC or New York. His real home was Lincoln, Nebraska.

As Zeke made his way through the security at the airport, he noticed a couple of people staring at him.

"I know you," one man said. "I saw you on the *Jack Cong* show."

"Yep, that was me," said Zeke.

"Where you headed?" asked the man.

"DC," replied Zeke.

"Those crooks," said the man. "You show 'em what for, son."

"You got it," said Zeke.

Within two and a half hours, Zeke was deboarding at Reagan National. He grabbed his carry-on luggage and walked toward baggage claim and then exited to hail a cab.

"Where to?" asked the cabbie.

"Silver Spring," replied Zeke, and he gave his home address.

When Zeke arrived at his home in Silver Spring, he showered and put on a suit for the interview. He decided that it probably would not be good to go on an interview on an empty stomach, so he fixed himself a late breakfast.

When he finished, he went out to his car, put in the address that Abby texted him into Waze and followed it which took him to I-495 West towards Frederick, Maryland and then past Potomac, Maryland into Virginia to the George Washington Memorial Parkway. The drive was very relaxing, actually a scenic route. Trees lined both sides of the parkway with their red, green, orange, and yellow leaves of fall. Stone overpasses partially hidden by the trees created a Harry Potter like feel as if he were travelling to a mysterious mansion. Or maybe it was just his anticipation of visiting this clandestine government facility which had been the subject of so many novels and movies.

Gradually, the trees opened up and he saw the Potomac River on the left. Cyclers appeared on the trails paralleling the river. He saw a guy rowing a canoe down the Potomac while a 747 airliner flew overhead along the path of the river. This was a side of DC that Zeke had not seen before. For a moment, he forgot that he was heading to the most clandestine agency in the country. And, he had yet to learn that he'd just been exposed to one of the survival secrets of life in Washington, DC, taking the time to enjoy the scenery in the midst of the chaos.

Zeke proceeded until he saw the CIA exit which he took. When he arrived at the guard station, Zeke told them that he was there for an interview. They asked him for his social security number and ran a quick check on it before letting him in and directing him to the visitor lot. After parking his car, Zeke proceeded to the main entrance. The windows of the building appeared to be tinted green. He figured it was to keep out the sunlight. Zeke passed through security on his way into the building. He told them that he was there for an interview with Agent Thomas Johnson, who security called.

"Mr. Johnson, we have a visitor to see you," said security. While waiting, Zeke noticed the CIA emblem and a verse from the Bible engraved in the floor. "And ye shall know the truth and the truth shall make ye free." John 8:32.

When Agent Johnson arrived in the lobby, he greeted Zeke. "Hi, Zeke. My name is Agent Thomas Johnson. Abby Sorensen has told me a lot about you. Abby interviewed extensively with us a couple of years ago. I regret that she did not come on board. She and the FBI were a better fit, I guess. They've got that squeaky-clean image, and they're a lot less covert than we are. Some people think that because we represent the American people, we are squeaky clean in everything we do. Reality is that we require our recruits to be squeaky clean before we corrupt them. That's a joke, son. Well, kinda. We often work with some unsavory characters. That's why we did not dismiss you out of hand when we heard about your past. A criminal record is an immediate disqualifier in most cases. But, first, Zeke, let me ask you, why do you want to work for the CIA?"

Zeke looked over at the verse engraved in the floor and pointed to it. "That's why."

"Good answer," said Agent Johnson. "Director Dulles would have applauded you. That engraving was put there by Allen Dulles, the fifth director of the CIA appointed by President Eisenhower. Follow me. I reserved a conference room where we can talk."

They walked up a flight of stairs and proceeded through a winding hallway of offices.

"This is the vault. Some people call it a SCIF or a Sensitive Compartmented Information Facility. I have the combination to it." Zeke looked confused. "Not exactly your typical office setting," commented Agent Johnson. "Everything is done on purpose for security. From the green tint on the windows to prevent outside electromagnetic monitoring to the combination locks on our office vaults to winding hallways that choke off radio transmissions. Secrecy is paramount."

Agent Johnson entered the combination and opened the vault. They took a seat.

"So, Zeke," said Agent Johnson. Talk to me. Tell me about yourself, including your arrest for that bomb scare when you were fourteen. Oh, by the way, I should mention that this interview is being recorded."

"OK. I plan on telling you everything," said Zeke.

"This is not our normal procedure, but you're not a normal candidate," said the agent. "But that's what we like to hear. You keep that mindset and you will do well here."

Zeke recounted his life to the agent as if he were his closest confidant. He told him all about the bomb scare and the deaths of the two teachers. He told him his real name. He told him of his time in the service and his time in college. Then, he told him about his time in DC and in New York and the revelation of his special gift.

"Several other agents and I have watched your interviews. That's why we're interested in you. You could be a great asset to the agency. Tell me, Zeke, do you think this gift is for real?"

"I don't know why I have it. It's not something I ever wanted. But it is real, and I'm starting to believe that God could use it to do good."

"Well, you'll have a chance to demonstrate it later in the process. I'll take this conversation back to all involved parties, and we'll discuss. Meanwhile, I want you to go about your daily business, but go online and update your SF-86 clearance forms to include all the information about the bomb scare and anything else you think we should know, especially drug usage. Make sure you include any incident in which your name has been entered on a police blotter. We will take it from there. Abby told me that the FBI suspended your current clearance. Don't worry about that. I understand that the security clearance attorney filed a motion to dismiss the application, and that the FBI agreed. That means you get a do-over. When you submit the updated SF-86, it will be processed as a new application. Give me a call when you've done that. I must warn you. We are going to put you through an extensive background check, full-scope polygraph, and psychological suitability evaluation. We look at your whole life and your lifestyle. As part of your evaluation, we're going to send you to a facility out in California where there are some researchers we use from time to time who will analyze and classify your ability. You'll be out there three to five days. I'll let you know when I've made the arrangements."

Agent Johnson stood up and shook Zeke's hand. "Good luck, Zeke. I hope to see you working for the CIA." Both men left the room and the agent escorted Zeke back to the lobby.

"Thanks for taking the time to meet with me," said Zeke before exiting the lobby. Zeke drove off the 256-acre compound wondering what it would be like to work for an organization so cloaked in secrecy. He found his way to the George Washington Memorial Parkway and drove towards I-495. Again, he noticed various cyclers on paths paralleling the main road. Such an idyllic setting amidst such chaos.

Zeke hurried home and began updating his SF-86 just like Agent Johnson told him taking care not to withhold any pertinent information. He was not sure what the future might hold, but he didn't want to blow what he thought was a second chance.

Later that evening he got a call from Abby Sorensen. "Zeke, how did it go? Did you have the interview with Agent Johnson? Zeke, I don't think you have anything to worry about. I investigated you first, remember? Other than the bomb scare incident, you look pretty clean to me, and you were fourteen when that happened, unless there's something else you're not telling me."

"No," replied Zeke. "That's the only thing."

"So then, relax and just wait."

"Oh, I do need to call him and tell him that I've finished the update," said Zeke.

"Yeah, do that," said Abby, "and keep me posted."

"Abby," said Zeke. "Would you…"

"Would I what?" asked Abby.

"Never mind. It was just an unfinished thought," said Zeke.

"Well, Zeke, when you finish your thought, call me back," said Abby. "Have a good day at the station tomorrow, and don't let them know what's going on."

"Not a chance," said Zeke.

After talking with Abby, Zeke called Agent Johnson. "Agent Johnson, this is Zeke Jackson. I hope I'm not calling too late."

"No, you're fine, Zeke."

"I wanted to let you know that I updated my SF-86."

"Wow. You got right on that. That's great, Zeke. I'll start the ball rolling from our end. An agent will be assigned to investigate you. When your SF-86 checks out, then we'll call you in for the poly. Then, if you pass the poly, we'll send you out to California for an eval, and after that we'll ask you for a demonstration of your ability. Meanwhile, sit tight and stay out of trouble."

"You got it," replied Zeke.

"Talk to you soon," replied Agent Johnson.

Zeke felt exhausted. It reminded of the tiredness he felt back in college during a serious bout of meningitis. He slept well that night.

The next morning, when he arrived at the station, Zeke skipped up the long set of white stone steps leading to the arched entrance. Once inside, he was greeted by Julie.

"Well, you're sure in a good mood this morning. Saw you coming up the steps. What's going on?"

"Nothing. Just got some clarity on some things," said Zeke. "How about lunch today?"

"Thanks, but I don't think so," replied Julie.

Zeke took the stairs up to the second floor and stopped by the coffee room before checking in with Harvey. Ellie from social media saw him and alerted him to a breaking story gaining traction on social media.

"Zeke, there's another demonstration planned for late this morning at the White House and the word on the street is that it's going to be more than a demonstration this time."

"What are they demonstrating against?" asked Zeke.

"Oh, you know, the usual: sexism, racism, poverty, destruction of the environment, affordable health care, a living wage. Hey, the sun is shining in old DC. That either means it's spring and the tourists are here, or it's a good day for a protest. Gotta get it in before the weather turns cold."

"Well," said Zeke. "I better see what Harvey wants me to do."

"Zeke," shouts Harvey. "Get in here. Sorry about your aunt. I had a favorite aunt, too. Hey, no hard feelings, I hope, about some of that stuff I said before you left. Sometimes, I can be very callous. It's an occupational hazard. You ready to go back to work?"

"Yeah, why not," said Zeke.

Harvey glanced at him with a brief questioning stare, before proceeding to give him his assignment.

"I want you and Sly to take a crew down to the White House entrance. The demonstrators are going to stage a protest at eleven am. I've gotta warn you. This time it might get physical, so pull back and let the police do their job. But keep the video rolling. Try to get some interviews with protestors, police, and whoever else might be there. Good luck and be safe."

Zeke found Sly in his cube and they both went downstairs and got a camera crew, packed up the van, and headed for the White House. On the way they watched some of the highlights of Sunday's Redskins game. In a way, the team had become emblematic of all that DC stood for, a new crop of rookies for a hopeful new year, but the same old losing game. They could make an all-star player look bad, not an easy team for a fan to love. But with the turning of the leaves and a nip in the air, it was a welcome distraction from the political scene.

When they arrived at 1600 Pennsylvania Avenue, or at least as close as they could get, there were already demonstrators gathering outside the wrought-iron fence in front of the White House. They were erecting a life-size stuffed doll of the president on a hangman's platform and placing a noose around its neck. A few Capitol Police were watching in the background but not interfering. It was an ominous sight but not an unfamiliar one.

Zeke got out of the van and began interviewing one of the demonstrators on camera. "Sir, what do think of the mock hanging? Do you think the president deserves this?"

"Every president gets at least one mock hanging," said the demonstrator. "Just consider it a 'Welcome to DC' celebration and we're the Welcoming Committee."

"Aren't you worried about being charged with a hate crime against the president?" asked Zeke.

"Hey, freedom of speech, man," said the demonstrator. "I'm a civil liberties lawyer. I know my rights."

It wasn't long before a couple hundred people had gathered. The demonstrator standing on the hangman's platform picked up a microphone and began talking to the crowd.

"This president has done away with pollution regulations in our country, so oil companies can frack our land and drill on our shorelines and our protected national parks. He has reduced taxes for the wealthy and raised them on working people. He has promoted racism by encouraging white supremacists. He's used waterboarding against Al-Qaeda terrorists violating their human rights. For these reasons and many more, we say rise up and take your country back."

Then, he climbed the wrought-iron fence, yelling, "Follow me," as he dropped inside the White House grounds. Other demonstrators, then, ran to the fence and climbed it, dropping inside the White House grounds. Almost immediately, they were met by at least a dozen Secret Service agents. FBI agents were also on hand. USSS Uniformed Division officers tackled and cuffed the demonstrators who had been wrestled to the ground.

A Secret Service agent got a megaphone and announced, "This demonstration is over. The demonstrators who have scaled the fence will be arrested and charged. Disperse immediately."

The demonstrators left the hangman's platform and ran away from the police. Sly, Zeke, and their camera crew kept shooting.

"Let's get a close up of the hangman's platform and the doll," said Sly.

"Another unpeaceful demonstration about the president," said Zeke on camera as he wrapped up the WJOP broadcast.

As Zeke was helping put away the broadcast equipment, a man in a suit walked up to him.

"Hi Zeke," said CIA Agent Johnson. Zeke looked up in surprise.

"Agent Johnson, surprised to see you here. What brings you out?"

"Just keeping tabs on things. The Agency occasionally sends us out on little ventures to keep abreast of what's going on."

"I covered the last demonstration," said Zeke. "This one definitely got out of hand. I'm surprised they don't do something about that fence. I hear there've been several fence jumpers in the last few years. My mother could climb that thing."

"The Secret Service and The U.S. National Park Service are talking about it," said Agent Johnson. "Nothing happens around here without a whole committee. They don't want to diminish the attractive, friendly look of the people's house."

"Yeah, but did they ever consider what mock hangings and burnings of the president might do to the friendly atmosphere?"

"That's why they have Capitol Police, Metropolitan Police, Park Police, the Secret Service, FBI, and CIA all hanging around. It doesn't go unnoticed."

"I wonder what he thinks when he looks out the window and sees a hangman's noose around his neck," said Zeke.

"Who? The president?" asked Agent Johnson.

"Yeah," said Zeke.

"This is DC, kid. The president doesn't have time for such nonsense. He knows that it's all part of the show. Look, I've got to go. Talk to you soon, Zeke."

"Glad I ran into you," said Zeke.

"Who's that?" asked Sly.

"Just a friend," replied Zeke.

After Sly, Zeke, and the camera crew packed up, they decided to stop for lunch at Meridian Hill Park, which was on their route back to the station. It was one of the lesser-known spots among tourists although very popular with the locals. They found a local street vendor, and they all got some food before heading to the park. Sly called Harvey to tell him that they were stopping for lunch.

"Harvey wants us to get some feature video while we're here," said Sly to the crew. "It's a 'stop and smell the roses' moment."

After they finished eating lunch, Sly suggested getting the video for Harvey. "Can you get a shot of the green lawn surrounded by the trees and their leaves changing color?"

"Sure thing," said the cameraman.

"This will make a nice feature piece," said Sly. "Put me on camera, guys, as I talk about the park."

"OK, Sly, I'll give you three. Three, two, one. You're on," said Zeke.

"This is Meridian Hill Park, so called because of its exact longitude with the original DC land marker. It's located on Sixteenth Street NW not far from the White House. The park has multiple names as I'll soon explain. It's one city block, designed like an Italian Garden, known for its mini bridges, waterfalls, luxurious green lawns, and the famous Sunday Drum Circle. More popular among locals than out-of-towners. Some know it as Malcolm X Park. There was a big effort to rename the park after the 1968 riots, but Congress rejected it due to its having been officially named the James Buchanan Memorial

Park, after the fifteenth president of the United States. My favorite spot is of the waterfall in front of the mausoleum."

The crew walked over to the waterfall.

"This is a favorite marriage proposal spot in the park which is also the home to many outdoor weddings. Hope you enjoyed our little fall diversion. For WJOP, this is Sly McDonald."

"Nice job," said Zeke.

"I like feature stories better than hard news," said Sly. "If it was up to me, I would only do feature stories."

The crew returned to the station which was only about ten minutes away. The camera crew unpacked the truck while Zeke and Sly went up to see Harvey.

"Hey, Boss, we got some feature footage for you," said Sly.

"What did you think of our live coverage of the demonstration?" asked Zeke.

"Nothing special," said Harvey. "What do you want, kid? An award? Come on over here. I'll pin a smiley face on ya. Look, I asked you guys for some real stuff on this assassination plot that I keep hearing about, but neither of you guys has given me much of anything. All you come up with is this tiptoe through the tulips stuff. We're a hard news station, not the *Oprah Winfrey Show*. Now, both of you guys, call up your contacts. See what you can do."

"OK, Boss," said Sly. "We'll do our best."

"Zeke," said Sly. "Why don't you call the FBI agents that interviewed you and see if they've heard anything?"

"I already did," replied Zeke. "They're not talking. This may be a long shot, but how about if we talk to the person who organized the two protests at the White House?"

"Do you think the demonstration has something to do with the assassination plot?" asked Sly.

"I don't know. I figure, where there's smoke, there's fire. I'll call the Secret Service at the White House and see if they still have that guy at the microphone in custody," said Zeke.

"Good idea," replied Sly.

Zeke called the Secret Service Media Relations Office, told them he was with WJOP, and inquired about the arrest of that morning's demonstrators scaling the White House fence.

They told him that all demonstrators who scaled the fence had been charged and released. They would eventually have to appear in local DC court. They agreed to send him a list of names of the demonstrators charged.

After about an hour, Zeke saw the list of names in his email. There were ten names, six men, four women. Zeke and Sly divided up the six men and ran background checks on them. Zeke discovered that one man on his list, Abdul Muti Poya, was an Afghani with ties to the Taliban. He told Sly, and they went downstairs to the studio to watch some of the video from the morning's demonstration. Sure enough, the lead demonstrator was Abdul Muti Poya. They had an address for the guy, so they told Harvey what they found.

"That's what I'm paying you guys for. Good work. Now, take a camera crew over there and interview the guy. Careful not to scare him off, though. People get weirded out when they see a WJOP camera van rolling up to their house."

Zeke and Sly went downstairs to the studios and got a one-man camera crew together. They loaded the van and Sly drove. Zeke observed dozens of students with books walking and riding bikes.

"Where are all these students going?" asked Zeke.

"Oh, University of Maryland is just up ahead," replied Sly. "My alma mater. I was too young to see it, but rumor has it that they would always block this road in the spring."

"What for?" asked Zeke.

"It was part of the coursework in the Philosophy Department. 'How to Form a New Mantra for the Nation and Promote It.' Blocking Route One was a sure way to get attention of both the state and federal lawmakers. No, I'm just kidding, but not about blocking the road. There was always some reason: Vietnam War, Richard Nixon, etc. One year in the early seventies, they had to close the school and put the campus under National Guard curfew because the student unrest got so bad. Oh, look over to the right. That's the University of Maryland Marching Band practicing on the chapel front lawn."

"Very beautiful campus," commented Zeke.

"It sure is," said Sly. "Huge too. It's about thirteen hundred acres and, as a student, you do a lot of walking."

They drove past the campus. About two miles down Route 1, they came to Riverside Apartments.

"He's in apartment 201," said Zeke.

"OK, guys. Zeke and I'll go up first. John, we'll call you when we want you to come up. Let's go, Zeke."

They knocked on the door several times before someone shouted, "Who is it?"

"Is this the residence of Abdul Muti Poya?" asked Zeke.

"Who wants to know?" asked the man.

"We are from WJOP," said Zeke. "I'm Zeke Jackson, and this is my coworker Sly McDonald. We were at the demonstration earlier and want to ask you some questions about your protest."

"I guess," said Abdul. "Anything for the cause." Abdul opened the door and let them in.

"You don't mind if we record this do you?" asked Sly before he turned on his inconspicuous pocket recorder.

"No, I guess not," replied Abdul.

"Did you organize the demonstration?" asked Zeke.

"Yes, I did," said Abdul.

"How about the one before that?"

"Look, I organize all protests. OK?"

"So, what is the name of your group?" asked Sly.

"The Four Point Front," said Abdul. "We're against sexism, racism, poverty, and destruction of the environment."

"Well, that seems reasonable," said Zeke. "Who would be for any of that stuff?"

"Well, well," said Abdul. "You're a comrade. You should join us in our fight."

"But I don't go around burning or hanging images of the president," replied Zeke.

Abdul extended a handshake to Zeke, and Zeke wasted no time taking it and looking him in the eye. Zeke saw that not only did Abdul have no armor, but a snake-like thing was coiled around him. Its reptilian scales blended into the black color of his shirt and pants permeating his whole body with a scaly, reptilian appearance. It had three raptor-like heads that sat above Abdul's head and hissed at Zeke.

"Who are you?" asked Zeke.

"We are Legion," the creature verbalized using Abdul's voice.

"A legion of demons?" asked Zeke.

"That we are."

"What do you want with Abdul?" asked Zeke.

"He belongs to us. He is our servant. He is on mission," replied the creature.

"What mission?" asked Zeke.

"You know," replied the creature.

"Be gone from him," commanded Zeke.

"We do not listen to you. You are weak and frail."

"In the name of the Lord Jesus Christ, be gone," commanded Zeke once again.

"We know who the Lord of Hosts is, but do you?" replied the creature.

Zeke backed off. Was the creature right? Did he know the Lord? The creature was questioning his faith. He would have to command a more powerful presence in the face of this demon. Zeke bowed his head for a brief moment asking the Lord to intervene. Afterward, Zeke followed up with a few more questions directed at Abdul and not the demon in possession. "Who supports your group? What organization?"

"I tell you, we are Four Point Front. We have no backers," said Abdul. "Anymore you talk to Janice Davies."

"Who is Janice Davies?" asked Zeke.

"Our riot organizer," replied Abdul.

"Do you have ties to the Taliban?" asked Zeke.

The creature reared its three heads and they all hissed viciously at Zeke.

"Why do you ask this? I am not terrorist. Enough questions. Are you police?"

"No, no," said Zeke. "We're WJOP News. Our truck is outside. Look out the window."

Zeke looked out the living room bay window and saw the camera van with WJOP written on the side, but he also saw an unmarked car with men in it.

"You may be news, but you brought cops with you. I recognize that car. It's been following me. You go now."

"We didn't bring the cops. We assure you," said Sly.

"It doesn't matter. You go now!"

"OK," said Zeke. "Thanks for talking to us."

Sly stopped his recorder. Zeke and Sly left the building. "Why did I get the impression that you were talkin' to somebody besides Abdul?" asked Sly.

"I was," replied Zeke. "I was talkin' to a demon named Legion. He was controlling my access to Abdul."

"Weird, man. Really weird," exclaimed Sly.

Outside they saw the car that Abdul had mentioned. The driver lowered his heavily tinted window and called to Zeke. "Zeke, come over here. What are you doing here?" asked Agent Johnson.

"Agent Johnson," said Zeke. "WJOP sent us here to interview Abdul Muti Poya. He's the leader of this morning's demonstration."

"Yeah, I know who he is," replied Agent Johnson. "Zeke, hop in the car for a minute. I want to introduce you to someone."

Zeke looked over at Sly and the cameraman and shrugged his shoulder. "I'll only be a minute. Don't worry. I know this guy."

Zeke opened the back door and got in the car. He saw someone in the front passenger seat. "Zeke," said Agent Johnson, "this is Secret Service Agent Don LaDividico." The Secret Service agent extended his hand to Zeke.

"Be careful, Don," said Agent Johnson. "Stuff can happen when you shake his hand. That's not just any hand."

"Oh yeah, I've heard about you," said Don. "You're that 'talk to me' guy."

"Is that what they call me now?" asked Zeke.

"Well, that's what they call you at the office."

"Sounds like I'm on somebody's radar," said Zeke.

"More than you know, kid."

"Well, nice to meet you," said Zeke. "I've got to go. Agent Johnson, I'm waiting."

"Yes, I know," said Agent Johnson. "Soon, it'll be soon. Hang in there."

"Until then," said Zeke.

Zeke got out of the car and went to the camera van. The cameraman was smoking outside the van. Zeke got into the van.

"What was that all about?" asked Sly.

"Nothing. He's just a friend," replied Zeke.

"You're hiding something from us," said Sly.

"And you, Sly. What are you hiding?"

"What do you mean?" asked Sly.

"You know exactly what I mean. You've done everything possible to sabotage my career at this station."

"No, that's not true," said Sly.

"You think I'm stupid or something?" asked Zeke. "And now, you want me to confide in you? Yeah, right. Give me your hand, Sly."

"Ah, no."

"I thought so. You're such a liar and cheat, and Harvey's not much better," said Zeke. "You and Harvey have been in this city so long that you've been assimilated into its sleaze. Let's just get back to the station."

The ride back to the station was quiet as they drove up Route 1. As they passed University of Maryland, the marching band was in full swing drilling its routines with the bandleader perched in his stand. They drove slow stopping for students as they crossed the street to the university bookstore.

"Oooo, Club LT" said Sly.

"What's the Club LT?" asked Zeke.

"The Little Tavern, students nicknamed it the Club LT, a favorite late-night stop for studiers and potheads with an appetite. You can easily down three or four of those little burgers. I'm going in," said Sly. "You guys interested?"

"No thanks," said Zeke and the cameraman.

While Sly went into the little restaurant, Zeke and John talked.

Sly returned to the van with a bag of burgers and a cup of coffee, and they resumed their ride back to the station. Once they arrived, Julie told them that Harvey wanted to see them right away.

"Well, what did you guys get?" asked Harvey.

"Abdul Muti Poya is definitely the demonstration organizer," Zeke told him. "The name of the group he represents is called The Four Point Front".

"What does that mean?" asked Harvey.

"They're against sexism, racism, poverty, and destruction of the environment," said Zeke.

"Is that it?" asked Harvey.

"There is one thing, but it doesn't sound like much," said Zeke.

"Well, what is it?" asked Harvey.

"Abdul told us to talk to Janice Davies, their riot organizer."

"Well, get on it," said Harvey. "Did you get him on camera?"

"No, he got spooked when I asked him if he had ties to the Taliban but I got him on audio," said Zeke.

"He's got government officials watching him," said Sly. "Zeke knows them, but he won't say who they are."

"What? Zeke, if you know who they are, you owe me that information," said Harvey. "We'll discuss that later. Right now, I want you to interview Janice Davies as soon as possible. We need some movement on this and something tells me she might get us going. Go alone. No camera crew. Just a pad and pencil. Let's try this the old-fashioned way. We don't want to spook her."

"OK, Boss, I'm on it," said Zeke.

Janice Davies was on the list of demonstrators who had been arrested earlier. Zeke looked up her address. She lived in Forestville, MD off Pennsylvania Avenue just outside of southwest DC but inside the beltway. He drove an unmarked WJOP station car to her home by way of Pennsylvania Avenue. When he arrived, he walked up to the front door of the small single-family home and rang the doorbell. A heavy-set woman in her twenties answered the door.

"Yes, can I help you?"

"Are you Janice Davies?" asked Zeke. He could hear a dog barking in the background.

"Yes, I am. Who wants to know?"

"Hello, I'm Zeke Jackson with WJOP. I was covering the demonstration in front of the White House this morning. I talked to Abdul Muti Poya earlier today. He suggested I talk with you."

"Oh really? When did I become the spokesperson for the group?" asked Miss Davies under her breath.

"You mean for the Four Point Front?" asked Zeke who still heard it. The barking was getting louder, but he could not see the dog. He could hear the dog scratching something.

"Well, that's the only group I know," she replied. "Come in." She extended a handshake to Zeke. "Don't worry about the dog. He's harmless. Besides, he's in the bedroom with the door closed."

Zeke quickly reciprocated making eye contact. He did not see any armor, and he did not see any demons. From his experience with this gift, he considered her to be neutral. So, he decided right then and there to refer to her type as a neutron. He would find no resistance to his questioning. Also, she owned no faith.

"So, are you the riot organizer?" he asked.

"Yes," she replied.

"What does that mean?" asked Zeke.

"Whenever a demonstration is supposed to get physical, I hand out certain weapons to certain people. I'm in charge of procuring and coordinating those weapons."

"Who do you procure the weapons from?"

"Different people."

"Who is your main go to?" asked Zeke.

"Ron Burch," responded Miss Davies.

"Who is Ron Burch?" asked Zeke.

"Weapons procurement," answered Miss Davies.

The German shepherd came running out the bedroom and jumped on Zeke breaking his handshake with Janice and knocking Zeke to the floor.

"Who?" asked Zeke as he got up not fully realizing his lock had broken.

"I don't know," replied Miss Davies. "Did I just tell you where I get the weapons? You tricked me. You tricked me," she said. "I know you. You're that guy. That mind reader. You need to go now. If Abdul ever finds out that I told you, he will have me killed."

"Miss Davies, he will never find out from me. I protect my sources."

It was late and it had been a long day. Zeke returned to his house in Silver Spring.

The next day Zeke returned to the station. He went right up to see Harvey and briefed him on the conversation with Miss Davies.

Then the conversation turned back to the one they were having before Zeke left to interview Miss Davies.

"Zeke, what government officials was Sly talking about yesterday?"

"I really can't say," replied Zeke.

"You owe me that information," said Harvey.

"What do you mean, I owe you?" asked Zeke. "I would tell you if I could, but I'm just not at liberty to say."

"You ungrateful little upstart," said Harvey. "After all I've done for you."

"What have you done for me, Harvey?"

"I gave you a job when you could barely speak," said Harvey. "I made you an icon in this town. I gave you opportunities at BlackRock that others would die for. I can't help that you're so set in your ways that you can't see what you've been given."

"I'll tell you what you did for me," said Zeke. "I came to work for this station with a solid track record for investigating and writing news. Instead of making me a better newsman, you made me a carnival side show. I can't walk down the street without someone ogling me and pointing their finger at me like they just saw Bigfoot. All I ever aspired to was to be like some of the great newsmen of the past: Walter Cronkite, Edward

R. Morrow, Woodward and Bernstein. And then, instead of supporting me in getting a clearance, you two sabotaged me and gave me a black eye with the FBI."

"You brought that on yourself," said Harvey.

"Maybe so," admitted Zeke, "but you two orchestrated the worst-case scenario."

"We had nothing to do with it," said Harvey.

"Come on. I may be a naive, but I'm not stupid," said Zeke. "Look, here's the deal. I got an inside track on this assassination thing, but I can't tell you anything. If it gets to the point when and where I can tell you something, you'll be the first to know. Until then, just keep my paycheck coming, and I'll do your news assignments."

"Well, well, kid," Harvey replied as he reached in his desk and pulled out a bottle of scotch filling two shot glasses and handing one to Zeke. "Congratulations! You finally got your head in the game. All right, I'll fund your little government venture, at least for the time being, but I'm expecting a payoff."

Zeke sipped the scotch from the shot glass.

"That's not how ya do it. This is how you do it," said Harvey, who quickly downed the shot.

Then, Zeke did the same but choked and coughed.

Harvey laughed. "You're a teetotaler," he said.

7

The Polygraph

Suddenly, Zeke's cell phone rang.

"Zeke, this is Agent Johnson."

"Hold on, sir," said Zeke recovering from the scotch. "Harvey, I've got to take this."

"Go ahead, kid," said Harvey. Zeke left the office and walked downstairs and went outside.

"Agent Johnson, go ahead, sir," said Zeke.

"Zeke, are you alone?" asked Agent Johnson.

"Yes," replied Zeke.

"Your SF-86 checks out. We want you to come in for a poly."

"When?" asked Zeke.

"Tomorrow morning, ten am. Now, Zeke, remember, just be honest even if it's uncomfortable. It's the polygrapher's job to ask questions that make you feel uncomfortable. We all have secrets. If you tell us yours, and you're a good fit which I think you are, then you're in. Get used to the polygraphs. CIA likes them a lot. We are bypassing the usual procedure and fast-tracking you because we have an immediate need for your particular skill."

"When do I get to demonstrate my supernatural gift?" asked Zeke.

"After you pass the polygraph and eval. We know you have it. We've seen you on TV. We'll want to see it firsthand to explore it further. Good luck, Zeke."

"Thanks," said Zeke. "I won't disappoint you."

After the call from Agent Johnson, Zeke called Harvey and told him he couldn't come in tomorrow because of some business he had with his government contacts. Then, Zeke decided to leave for the day.

The ride home only took about ten minutes but seemed like an eternity as Zeke pondered all the embarrassing things he could be asked. He wondered why he would allow himself to be put under such scrutiny. He thought back to the walk in Wilderness Park and what the pastors said about his special gift. They had concluded that it was a supernatural ability given to him by the Holy Spirit for some inexplicable reason. They both thought it was legit. Zeke took much solace in this. After pulling into his parking lot, he sat in the car staring at the bright sun. With his hands still grasping the steering wheel, he bowed his head in prayer.

"Lord, it's been a long time. I've been trying to do things my way, and in the process, I've lost my way. I've forgotten where I came from, and most of all I've forgotten you and your ways. I doubted who you are. No more doubting. I'm tired of doing things my way. I feel so empty. Lord Jesus, I believe you are who you say you are, the Son of the living God. I believe you died for my sins and arose from the grave. I want to do things your way. Instruct and guide me, Lord, from here on out. And, Lord I don't know why you gave me this supernatural ability. I don't understand it, but this government agency wants to use it. I commit to be truthful with them and let the chips fall where they may. Lord, be with me tomorrow. And, by the way, thanks for my great parents and Aunt Becky who love me and are always interested in my spiritual welfare."

After his prayer, Zeke called Abby.

"Abby, this is Zeke. Guess what?"

"They called you to come in," replied Abby.

"That was a good guess," said Zeke.

"An investigator called me a couple days ago asking about you," replied Abby. "I figured it would be happening soon."

"Thanks for letting me know," said Zeke facetiously.

"Not that I didn't want to," said Abby, "but, it's better that I didn't. Don't want to show any bias."

"I go in tomorrow morning at ten for a polygraph."

"Don't worry about it, Zeke. You'll do fine. I know first-hand that these things can be intimidating. Just tell them the truth."

"Yeah, that's what Agent Johnson said."

"Zeke, he's on your side. He wants you in there and so do I," said Abby.

"Abby, thanks," said Zeke.

"Oh, by the way, don't drink any coffee in the morning," said Abby.

"Why?" asked Zeke.

"Don't worry about it. You'll thank me later."

"OK," said Zeke.

Zeke went into his house, had a light dinner, and watched the evening news and a couple of game shows before going to bed. He set his alarm for 7:30 am. The traffic would probably be bad next morning and he would need to allow a good hour for the commute. He fell asleep like he had just been given a dose of sodium pentothal and woke up surprised when the alarm clock went off.

What happened to the night? he thought.

As he got out of bed, he felt the cold of an early November morning. He had not yet turned on the heat. After showering and shaving, he made some coffee and some bacon and eggs and ate breakfast. Remembering what Abby told him, he decided not to drink the coffee. Instead, he had some orange juice. After breakfast, he brushed his teeth and put on a suit. He noticed it was 8:30, so he went to his car. A light frost covered the windows, so he started the car and removed the frost with a scraper.

He followed Waze which again took him to I-495 West towards Frederick, Maryland and then past Potomac, Maryland into Virginia where he encountered traffic stopped and waiting to cross the Cabin John Bridge. Gradually, the traffic loosened up causing him a thirty-minute delay. Zeke took the George Washington Memorial Parkway and proceeded until he saw the CIA exit which he took.

When he arrived at the guard station, Zeke again told them he was there for an interview. They asked him for his social security number and ran a quick check on it before letting him in and directing him to the visitor lot.

After parking his car, Zeke proceeded to the main entrance. He again noticed the green windows. Zeke passed through security on his way into the building. He told them that he was there for an interview with Agent Thomas Johnson. Security called Agent Johnson.

"Agent Johnson, we have a visitor to see you," said security.

"Zeke," said Agent Johnson, "How was your ride in?"

"Lost about thirty minutes getting over the Cabin John Bridge," said Zeke.

"What's new?" replied Agent Johnson. "Well, are you ready for this?"

"I think so," replied Zeke.

"Like I told you yesterday, just be truthful. They'll try to rattle you. Remain calm."

Zeke laughed.

"What's so funny?" asked Agent Johnson.

"I don't know," replied Zeke. "I just had a thought. I was wondering if this is what it's going to be like on judgement day for those who don't know God."

"Well," said Agent Johnson. "That's out of my wheelhouse, but I can tell you that this side of eternity, the CIA believes it is God."

They walked upstairs to a room with a polygraph examiner and his machine and several armed guards in the room. One had a gun. Zeke took a seat, and they connected him to the machine.

Zeke looked the examiner in the eye and said, "Give me your hand. I'll take over now."

Laughter came from behind the one-way glass window overlooking the room.

"That's funny," said the stoic examiner. "I hope you are still laughing by the time this is over. Now, I want you to answer my questions with a yes or no only."

"Yes, sir," said Zeke.

"Is your birth name Zeke Jackson?" asked the examiner.

"No," replied Zeke.

"Is your birth name Joseph Black?"

"Yes," replied Zeke.

"Is Zeke Jackson your real name?"

"Yes," replied Zeke.

"Were you born in 1995?"

"Yes," replied Zeke.

"Did you drive here this morning?"

"Yes," replied Zeke.

"Would your friends characterize you as a truthful person?"

"Yes," replied Zeke.

"Are you willing to betray your government in the name of government?"

Zeke pondered the question for about thirty seconds and answered, "Yes."

"Have you ever taken drugs?"

"Yes," replied Zeke.

"Were you born in Lincoln, Nebraska?"

"Yes," replied Zeke.

"Did you drink coffee this morning?"

"No," replied Zeke.

"Have you ever had sex with an animal?"

"That's disgusting," replied Zeke.

"Just answer yes or no," said the examiner.

"No," replied Zeke.

"Have you ever had sex with a minor?"

"Again, disgusting," replied Zeke.

"Again, yes or no," said the examiner.

"No," replied Zeke.

"Have you ever committed a crime other than a minor traffic violation?"

"Yes," replied Zeke.

"Was the crime the bomb scare when you were a minor?"

"Yes," replied Zeke.

"Were you arrested?"

"Yes," replied Zeke.

"Other than the bomb scare, is there any other crime, excluding minor traffic violations, that you have committed?

"No," replied Zeke.

"Was anyone injured in that bomb scare?"

"Yes," replied Zeke.

"Did two teachers die as a result of that bomb scare?"

"No," replied Zeke.

"Did you do six months in juvie as a result?"

"Yes," replied Zeke.

"So again, I ask you. Did two teachers die as a result of that bomb scare?"

"No," replied Zeke.

The examiner looked at his machine and determined there was no indication of deception. He rephrased the question.

"Did two teachers have heart attacks as they were leading their students from the school building in response to the bomb scare?"

"Yes," replied Zeke.

"Were you charged with manslaughter because of the deaths of those two teachers?"

"Yes," replied Zeke.

"Were you acquitted of these charges?"

"Yes," replied Zeke.

"Did you actually plant a bomb at the high school?"

"No," replied Zeke.

"Were you charged with the crime of reckless endangerment?"

"Yes," replied Zeke.

"We're you found guilty of this crime?"

"Yes," replied Zeke.

"Were you sentenced to six months in juvie for this crime?"

"Yes," replied Zeke.

"Was this crime later expunged from your record?"

"Yes," replied Zeke.

"Do you have a psychic ability to make people tell the truth?"

"No," replied Zeke.

"Did you tell Agent Johnson that you had a psychic ability to make people tell the truth?"

"No," replied Zeke.

"Did you tell Agent Johnson that you had the ability to make people tell the truth?"

"Yes," replied Zeke.

"Do you do it through extrasensory perception?"

"No," replied Zeke.

"Can you predict the future?"

"No," replied Zeke.

"Do you consider this ability to be supernatural in nature?"

"Yes," replied Zeke.

"So would you say that you have a supernatural ability to make people tell the truth?"

"Yes," replied Zeke.

"Let's take a break," said the examiner. "Zeke, the guards will escort you to the restroom. We'll resume when you get back."

The guards disconnected Zeke from the machine and escorted him down the hall to the restroom.

Meanwhile, Agent Johnson stepped into the examination room. "How's he doing?" he asked the examiner.

"No deception so far," responded the examiner. "The rest of this is just verifying what he's put on his security forms. Unless he's hiding something there, I don't think we have a problem. We already knew about the bomb scare."

"I better get back to the observation room," said Agent Johnson.

When Zeke returned with the guards by his side, they connected him up and continued the questioning for another two hours, but it was uneventful.

"Zeke," said the examiner. "We are done. I will leave you in the care of Agent Johnson. Thanks for coming in today."

After Agent Johnson walked into the room, Zeke impatiently asked him, "Did I pass?"

Agent Johnson looked at the examiner who was still in the room and asked, "Well, did he?"

The examiner looked at them both and said, "I still need to review the results more carefully, but I can tell you that I saw no deception."

Zeke breathed a sigh of relief. "I'm exhausted," he exclaimed.

"Well done, Zeke," said Agent Johnson. "Let's go, and I'll tell you what's next as I escort you out of the building."

"Can we lose the armed guards?" asked Zeke jokingly.

"You guys are dismissed," responded Agent Johnson with a smile.

As they walked down to the lobby, Zeke noticed their conversation becoming more open and revealing.

"Zeke, I wondered how you were going to handle it when the examiner asked you if two teachers died as a result of that bomb scare? I thought for sure I would hear the polygraph needle slamming the side of the machine. But I have to give you credit. Your answer was spot on. It forced the examiner to come at you from a different angle, and you didn't say yes until he rephrased the question to the way in which you could answer in the affirmative. Great job! I need to check with the examiner one more time to get him to submit his analysis. Then, I'll arrange for your California eval. This will happen fast, probably by tomorrow."

"OK," said Zeke. "I'll be ready."

Zeke left the building and started his drive home. His mind drifted so much that he hardly noticed the scenery. He had spent about five hours under a polygraph and had not even stopped for lunch. He was so tired that he did not even realize that he was hungry. The next thing he knew was that he was pulling into the driveway of his home. All he wanted to do was to go to bed, but he wanted to call Abby first and let her know how it went.

"Abby, this is Zeke."

"How did it go?" she asked.

"It went well," said Zeke. He proceeded to fill Abby in on the details. "Hopefully, Agent Johnson will call me tomorrow about my psychic eval. I'm going to bed now. I'm exhausted."

"Yeah, get some rest," replied Abby. "Great news."

"Abby," said Zeke. "When this is all over, we should celebrate."

"You got it," said Abby. "Now get some rest."

Zeke fell asleep and awoke the next morning to a call on his cell phone. "Zeke, this is Agent Johnson. Good news. You've been cleared to proceed. I booked you a flight to San Francisco International Airport (SFO) for later today at 3:10 pm EST and a hotel three miles from Menlo Park, California for psychic evaluation. You're to report to the lobby of Science and Research International Corporation (SRIC) in Menlo Park, California for testing at 8:00 am PST tomorrow."

After Zeke got out of bed, he called Harvey. "Harvey, my government contacts want me to go out of town for a few days for some testing."

"Look kid, you've got to give me something better than that. Do these government contacts work for the agency I think they work for?"

"Who do you think they work for?" asked Zeke.

"CIA, of course," replied Harvey.

"I can neither confirm nor deny," replied Zeke.

"So if you told me you would have to kill me?" asked Harvey.

"That's right," replied Zeke.

"OK, kid, go ahead, but when you get back, we've got to talk about a new arrangement. Think stringer. For now, I'll just consider you away on assignment."

"Hey, thanks Boss. It'll pay off for you in the end. Trust me," said Zeke.

"It better," said Harvey.

8

Psychic Spies

For nearly twenty years, the CIA had been researching and using something they called remote viewing based on psychic, clairvoyant ability. It gave them the ability to see remote places without actually being there. The CIA had some success using this but concluded that it had no value as an intelligence tool and ended the program in 1995.

Still, an appetite for it remained in the CIA, and they viewed Zeke's ability as a psychic phenomenon. So, as part of Zeke's onboarding process, the CIA wanted to evaluate him at Science and Research International Corporation (SRIC) in Menlo Park, California.

Zeke boarded a plane at Reagan National Airport at 3:10 pm EST bound for San Francisco International Airport. Zeke arrived in San Francisco at 5:00 pm PST, and was surprised at the cool sixty-degree November weather. He naively expected a minimum of eighty-degree temperatures year-round throughout all of California.

After renting a car at the airport, he drove to his hotel in Menlo Park. The next morning Zeke reported to SRIC. After entering the main lobby, he told security that he had been sent by Agent Johnson at Langley for psychic evaluation.

"Oh, you're Zeke Jackson. We were told to expect you. Dr. Powell will be right down."

After about ten minutes, Dr. Powell came down the stairs into the lobby. "Hello, Zeke. We've heard a lot about you. We're excited to have you here this week."

"We?" asked Zeke.

"Yes, my team. We have four people who will be working with you to determine the nature of this ability that you have. Come with me to our Remote Viewing Lab on the second floor."

When Zeke entered the Remote Viewing Lab, it was as if he had walked into Frankenstein's laboratory. Aisles of lab benches with electronic devices filled the room, their red, blue, and green LEDs blinking.

Zeke touched one of the devices. "What's this?"

"That's an EMF Detector," said Dr. Powell. "It's also known as a TriField Meter. It detects fluctuations in magnetic, electric, radio, and microwave energy levels."

"That's another name for a ghost detector," said Sean, one of Dr. Powell's assistants. "It's a ghost detector."

"Zeke, meet Sean Davidson," said Dr. Powell. He's our electronic tech here."

Zeke looked and touched another device. "How about this?"

"That's a Thermal Anomaly Detector," said Dr. Powell. "It detects small changes in thermal fields that can accompany paranormal phenomena."

"That's also another name for a ghost detector," said Sean. "It just detects thermal changes."

"Might I ask, what your doctorates are in?" asked Zeke.

"I have doctorates in parapsychology and paranormal science with a masters in physics," said Dr. Powell.

"So you're the chief ghostbuster," said Zeke.

"I guess you could say that, but that's not a term I like to banter about," said Dr. Powell. "We have enough trouble maintaining credibility around here."

Zeke spotted a cranial looking device with electrodes and wires hanging off. "What's that?" he inquired.

"That's what we're going to be putting on your head to monitor your brain waves when you're doing your thing," replied Sean "It's called an EEG Brain Wave Monitor. You can buy these things off Amazon now for like two hundred dollars, but they don't do what this does. Dr. Powell designed this himself. I know it looks kind of Frankenstein, but it monitors areas of the brain no other EEG monitoring devices can look at."

"OK, Sean, if you're done playing with the toys, take Zeke in the back room and hook him up to the EEG monitor," said Dr. Powell. "We'll start the testing there."

"OK, Boss."

The back room was much like the polygraph room at Langley. They had a one-way observation window, but they didn't have armed guards.

"This place is not quite as scary as Langley," said Zeke as he entered the room.

"OK, Zeke," said Sean. "Have a seat and get comfortable. I'm going to place this helmet on your head. It has several electrodes attached to it. You won't get shocked. Dr. Powell will be monitoring your brain waves on a fancy oscilloscope in the next room."

After Sean hooked Zeke up, Dr. Powell came into the room. "Zeke, I want you to interview Sean the same way you interviewed others on whom you exercised your gift. You choose the questions. I'll be in the next room. I can hear everything you say."

"OK, Sean, give me your hand," said Zeke. "Now make eye contact with me. You have no armor."

"OK," replied Sean.

"You are wandering in the woods searching for something," said Zeke. "Is your name Sean Davidson?"

"Yes," said Sean.

"Your heart is anxious and fearful. You're frustrated because you cannot find what you're looking for. What are you looking for, Sean? Sean, what are you looking for?"

"Forgiveness," answered Sean. "Forgiveness and God."

"Forgiveness for what, Sean?"

"For cheating on my girlfriend," answered Sean.

"Does she know?"

"No," answered Sean.

"How did you meet your girlfriend?"

"She was my girlfriend in high school," answered Sean.

"So, why don't you tell her and beg her forgiveness?"

"Because I cheated with her best friend," said Sean. "I feel so guilty."

"That's enough for now," said Dr. Powell over the intercom.

Zeke let go of Sean's hand. Dr. Powell came into the room and removed the helmet from Zeke's head. Sean appeared dazed but soon recovered. Dr. Powell asked Sean if he remembered telling Zeke about his girlfriend. Sean said he remembered telling him about his cheating.

"Zeke, great job," said Dr. Powell. "Just the kind of thing I was hoping to see."

"What happened on your scope?" asked Zeke.

"My scope showed your brain waves consistently between four and seven point nine hertz frequency. Your brain was in the alpha state, which is where the mind is relaxed, and 'in the zone.' Have you ever studied or practiced meditation?"

"No," replied Zeke.

"What I need is to see is what is happening to Sean's brain," said Dr. Powell. "I think we need to run the experiment again with an EEG helmet on Sean also. But for now, why don't we break for an early lunch."

"Sean," said Dr. Powell. "Why don't you gather the team together, and we'll take Zeke out to lunch."

"Where to?" asked Sean.

"How about that Caribbean restaurant that you guys love so much?"

"Great idea," said Sean.

As Sean gathered the team together, Dr. Powell and Zeke talked. "I hear that you don't think this is psychic," said Dr. Powell.

"No, I don't," said Zeke.

"What do you think it is, then?"

"I think it's supernatural or divine in nature."

"What do you mean by supernatural?" asked Dr. Powell.

"I think it is an ability or gift bestowed on me by the Holy Spirit, at this time, for some reason."

"You mean, like one of those gifts in the Bible, like speaking in tongues or healing?"

"Oh, you're familiar with them?"

"Yes, I would be remiss if did not do my homework on various forms of paranormal ability," said Dr. Powell. "We've investigated many of those claims and found them to be fraudulent. What makes you so sure that yours is the real deal?"

"Well, for one thing, I'm not trying to make money from it. I know there is an entire industry that has been built up around the proclamation of having these abilities," said Zeke. "And, there are around two hundred Christian evangelical denominations built around these gifts. They are the cause of much contention in the Christian community. Personally, I think these particular gifts of healing, miracles, and tongues were meant for the early church to give testimony to the Lord Jesus Christ and to identify the work of the Holy Spirit. I don't think they were meant to become a sales pitch for televangelists."

"Well, I'm with you there," said Dr. Powell. "I think the team is waiting for us. Let's go."

Zeke and Dr. Powell met the team in the lobby where Dr. Powell introduced him to all the members. "You know Sean, of course. Sean is our electronic tech. He has a B.S. in Electronic

Technology and fixes a lot of the equipment in this place. This is Marie Sanchez. She has a PhD in parapsychology, and is our senior researcher. This is Paul Mayers. Paul is our neurologist, M.D. specializing in..."

"Let me guess," interrupted Zeke. "The effects of psychic abnormalities on the brain."

"Exactly," said Dr. Powell. "And, last but not least, Jason Milford. Jason is our lead designer of paranormal and psychic detection and measuring equipment. He has a PhD in electrical engineering and a masters in biology."

"What a team," said Zeke. "Very highly educated."

"Now that we're done with the introductions, let's load into the ghostbusters' van and go to lunch," said Dr. Powell.

They walked out into the parking lot and Zeke saw a ridiculous looking van.

"You weren't kidding," said Zeke as he inspected the van decked out like the ghostbusters' vehicle.

"Yeah," said Dr. Powell. "It's good advertising for the company. We drive it in the Rose Bowl parade and in the homecoming parade for Stanford University with whom we're also affiliated. Most people think it's a joke, but, as you can see, we are very serious and so is SRIC. We have earned millions in government research and studies and mission critical operations. The CIA has tabled their support for now, but we feel it's only a matter of time before they come back to us."

Everyone loaded into the van and they drove a couple miles to the Back A Yard American and Caribbean Grill. The smell of jerk chicken greeted them at the door.

"What do you recommend here?" asked Zeke.

"Jerk chicken, of course," said Sean. "Can't you smell it? After that, it's all about the sides."

After sitting down, and looking at the menu, Zeke decided on the jerk chicken with white meat, collard greens, and rice and beans. The rest of the team went with the jerk chicken but varied on the sides.

"How long have you guys been working together?" asked Zeke.

"Marie and I started the group at SRIC about ten years. ago," said Dr. Powell. "Jason came about a year later. Then, Paul came three years after that. Sean is our newest member. He joined us a year ago. People in this field all know one another. We're a close-knit bunch."

After they finished eating, Dr. Powell spoke up, "Are you guys ready to get back at it?" Dr. Powell picked up the tab and they went out to the ghostbusters' van, and Dr. Powell drove them back to the office.

"Thanks for lunch, Boss," said Sean.

They all proceeded to the lab.

Dr. Powell, Sean, and Zeke went into the testing room inside the lab. This time Dr. Powell put his customized EEG helmet on Zeke and a duplicate on Sean before going to the observation room.

"OK, Zeke, you can begin," said Dr. Powell over the intercom.

Zeke grasped Sean's hand and looked him in the eye.

"You have no armor," said Zeke. "Again, you are wandering in the woods searching for something Your heart is anxious and fearful. What are you looking for, Sean? Sean, what are you looking for?"

"A way out," replied Sean.

"A way out of what?" asked Zeke.

"A way out of this relationship," said Sean.

"What relationship?" asked Zeke.

"The relationship with Heather."

"Who's Heather?"

"My girlfriend's best friend," admitted Sean.

"Why can't you end the relationship with Heather?" asked Zeke.

"She's threatening me."

"How is she threatening you?"

"She's threatening to tell my girlfriend. She knows I don't want to lose her."

Across the intercom came Dr. Powell's voice. "OK, enough secrets for today. Let's end the session."

Dr. Powell entered the room and removed the helmets from Zeke and Sean. Dr. Powell approached Zeke.

"I believe what you uncovered in there," Dr. Powell told Zeke.

"Yeah, but I'm getting tired of sniffing around everyone's dirty laundry. This gift has to be for something bigger than that," replied Zeke.

"I'm just glad it wasn't something illegal you uncovered," said Dr. Powell. "This ability that you have is uncanny. Tell me one thing, Zeke. On both interviews, you made the statement: 'You have no armor.' What did you mean?"

"The armor refers to the armor of God, a reference to the book of Ephesians in the New Testament," explained Zeke. "The fact that Sean did not have any armor means that he's susceptible to any and all attacks from the evil one. He has no defense or offense, for that matter. He is open to any temptation. From a spiritual perspective, he is wandering, lost and unprotected."

"But, what about self-control? What about being responsible for your actions?" asked Dr. Powell.

"He's certainly responsible for his actions," said Zeke. "'Make no mistake, your sin will find you out,' the Old Testament says. As far as self-control goes, without the Holy

Spirit and the armor of God, it's whatever he can muster up in his own ability. He has no help from God."

"But what about just being a decent and good person?" asked Dr. Powell. "Doesn't that count for something?"

"All goodness comes from God," replied Zeke. "No God, no goodness. If Sean has excluded God from his life, he lives a human existence in spiritual darkness."

"Well, Zeke, I don't agree with everything you're saying, but I find it very interesting. I can see why you claim your gift to be divine in nature. I still want to run some more tests on you. Let's call it quits for today, and I'll see you back here tomorrow morning at eight thirty am."

"OK," said Zeke. "And, I'm sorry to reveal Sean's personal troubles."

"It's his problem," replied Dr. Powell.

Zeke got an early dinner, returned to his hotel room, and went to bed early. The next morning, he showed up at the research facility at 8:30 am. He got a new visitor's badge and went up to the lab.

"Good morning, Zeke," said Dr. Powell. I want to test you on some remote viewing today. Have you ever done remote viewing?"

"No," said Zeke, "and I doubt that I can do it. I have no clairvoyant or psychic abilities."

"Well, I just want to see if you have the ability or even a penchant for it."

"OK," said Zeke. "I'll play along."

"We'll start very basically. I'm going to have Marie sit in another room and hold up some cards with pictures on them. You're going to be in the back room that you were in yesterday. When I say ready, I want you to focus on what you think Marie is holding up and sketch what you see or what you think you see." Dr. Powell put the EEG monitor helmet on him again, and went into the observation room. This time he asked Dr. Mayers, the neurologist, to join him.

"OK, Zeke, Marie is holding up the first card."

Zeke relaxed and fell asleep. Zeke went into a sleep REM state. A blurred image started to come through but then disappeared. Dr. Powell's special EEG monitor allowed him and Dr. Mayers to see the remote image as it came through the brain. But the image stopped and Zeke awoke and began drawing what he thought he saw. So, he began to draw something like a sword that ended up becoming a Christmas tree.

"OK, Zeke, Marie is holding the second card."

Again, Zeke relaxed and fell asleep. Again, Zeke went into a sleep REM state. A blurred image started to come through but then disappeared. When the image stopped, Zeke awoke and drew the outline of a person. He drew a picture of the Christ. Dr. Powell continued for a couple more cards, but the result was the same. Something always blocked the final image.

Zeke had enough. He started to remove the EEG helmet when Dr. Powell came in and offered to help.

"Dr. Mayers observed you going in and out of theta," said Dr. Powell. "Now, let me see what you've drawn."

As Dr. Powell looked at the drawings, he saw that none of them matched what Marie had been holding up. "I don't understand this," said Dr. Powell. "The images were coming through, and then they stopped. Something interrupted the transmission."

In an attempt to determine what interrupted the transmission, Dr. Powell brought Jason Milford, his psychic detection equipment designer, in to the same room as Zeke to monitor for electrical, magnetic, and radio interference. Dr. Powell reran one of the tests which yielded the same results.

"Any interference?" asked Dr. Powell.

"No electrical, magnetic, or radio interference," said Jason.

"Zeke," said Dr. Powell. "I'm going to my office. When you feel up to it, come and see me. I want to ask you some questions."

Zeke took five minutes to clear his head and then went to see Dr. Powell. Marie, Paul, and Jason were there also.

"Zeke, we are at a loss as to what is going on," said Dr. Powell. "Usually, if someone is not going to have a remote vision, he would see nothing or he might see something or someone familiar very clearly, which would indicate imagination. But you went into theta REM state which is indicative of remote viewing and actually started to see what was in the subject's hand, but you lost it. You lost the view. Jason monitored for possible interference but saw nothing. So, did you notice anything? Did you see or sense anything that would have interfered with the remote view?"

"Well," said Zeke, "I did see a shield come up."

"Oh, here we go again with the armor of God," said Dr. Powell.

"Well, that's what I saw," said Zeke.

"OK, what does the shield mean?"

"The Shield of Faith. It's used to extinguish the flaming missiles of the evil one."

"Who is the evil one?" asked Dr. Sanchez.

"Satan, Lucifer, of course," replied Zeke.

"So, are you saying that the information we wanted you to view was, in some way, from Satan?"

"I don't know," said Zeke. "But I do know this. The Holy Spirit didn't want me to remote view those items for some reason. If I had to conjecture, I would say that the Holy Spirit does not want me to engage in remote viewing. He does not want me using this gift for that."

"But he wants you to see and interpret people's spiritual states and extract the truth from them?" asked Dr. Powell.

"Yes," said Zeke. "Perhaps, He's given me this ability for some purpose that he wants to accomplish.

And that purpose is to help thwart the assassination plot on the president and vice president, thought Zeke.

"God's way of intervening in the affairs of men. Look, guys, I know you want to be able to figure out how I can do what I do. That way you can replicate it. Maybe teach it to other people like you teach remote viewing. Maybe market it to the government for some big contracts. But I think that what I have is a one-off. I'm one of a kind. So, why don't you just vouch for me and tell the CIA that I'm legit, but I'm not psychic."

"OK, Zeke," said Dr. Powell. "I'm going to tell Langley that you're a touch-enabled, real-time interactive, spirit-powered psychometric."

"I'm gonna take that to mean that I'm filled with the Holy Spirit," replied Zeke.

"Whatever you need to believe," said Dr. Powell.

"Does this mean we're done here and I can return to DC?" asked Zeke.

"Yes," said Dr. Powell. "Zeke, it's been a pleasure. Put in a good word for us at Langley."

The rest of the Remote Viewing team said their goodbyes.

"Don't worry, I'll talk you guys up at Langley." Zeke was a little miffed that Dr. Powell, with his awareness of spiritual gifts, didn't just agree that his ability was a divine gift.

Zeke thought of Pastor Jones, his older pastor, and wondered what he would think of all this. He still had his number. Anyway, he wanted to let him know of his recent recommitment to the Lord. So, after he left the building and got into his rental car, he called Pastor Jones.

"Pastor Jones, this is Zeke Jackson. I mean Joseph Black."

"Joseph, how are you? It's interesting that you called. God has put you on my mind, recently. I've been praying for you, especially, as you are living in that godless city, DC. What's happening with you?"

"Pastor, it's comforting to hear your voice. Thank you for praying for me. It is a dark city. It is a dark world."

"That's the truth," said Pastor Jones.

"Pastor, I came back to the Lord or should I say, I came to the Lord."

"Joseph, He just came to claim what was rightfully His to begin with. He chose us in Him before the creation of the world."

"Thank you, Pastor," said Zeke.

"No, thank you, Jesus, for what you've done for Joseph," said Pastor Jones.

"Amen," said Zeke.

"One more thing, Pastor. This thing I have."

"You mean your divine gift?" asked Pastor Jones.

"Yes. The government is looking to me to help them by using this gift. They sent me to a psychic lab to try to figure out what to call it. They say I'm a *touch-enabled, real-time, interactive, spirit-powered psychometric.*"

"A what?" asked Pastor Jones?

"A *touch-enabled, real-time, interactive, spirit-powered psychometric,*" chuckled Zeke.

"Leave it to the government to confuse what The Almighty has done. Joseph, I can't even say all that stuff, but you ain't that. You is Holy Ghost filled."

"Thank you, Pastor. That's what I told them, but I just needed to hear you say it."

9

Demoing the Gift

After Zeke wrapped up his psychic evaluation at the Remote Viewing Lab, he got a call from Agent Johnson. "How's it going, Zeke? Did you finish your eval?"

"Yes," Zeke replied. "They classified me as a touch-enabled, real-time interactive, spirit-powered psychometric."

"That's great," said Agent Johnson. "The Agency will be pleased. I'll book you a plane back to Washington this afternoon. Now, can you come to Langley tomorrow morning?"

"Yes," replied Zeke. "What time?"

"Ten o'clock," said Agent Johnson.

"No problem," replied Zeke.

The next morning, Zeke showered and dressed. Realizing how hungry he was, Zeke decided to get something into his stomach before leaving, so he fixed some toast and eggs and poured a glass of juice. He called Julie and told her to let Harvey know that he would not be coming in that day. After breakfast, Zeke got in the car and proceeded on his standard route to Langley, taking I-495 toward Frederick and around Potomac to the Cabin John Bridge. Again, he encountered a thirty-minute delay before getting on the George Washington Memorial Parkway. He proceeded until he saw the CIA exit which he took. When he arrived at the guard station, Zeke again told them that he was there for an interview. They asked him for his social security number and ran a quick check on it before letting him in and directing him to the visitor lot. After parking his car, Zeke proceeded to the main entrance. Zeke passed through security on his way into the building. He told them that he was there for an interview with Agent Johnson whom security called.

"Agent Johnson, we have a visitor to see you," said security.

When Agent Johnson saw Zeke in the lobby, he said to him, "I've arranged for some of the higher-ups to observe this demonstration. I also have some agents that were part of the old 'remote viewing' program, called Project Stargate."

"What's that?" asked Zeke.

"That's been declassified," replied Agent Johnson. "The CIA used to do research in the area of psychic ability to see things in distant locations without actually being there."

"My ability is not psychic. It's supernatural," replied Zeke.

"That's OK, Zeke. The CIA likes supernatural, too. Whatever gives us an edge," said Agent Johnson.

"Psychic ability is suspect," said Zeke. "You don't know where the power is coming from. It could be demonic in nature."

"Yeah, I know some people believe that," said Agent Johnson. "Usually people of faith. They shut the Stargate Program down many years ago, partially because of that. Anyway, I've arranged for you to interview a known person who we know much about. We want you to demonstrate that you can extract information from him. He's a Saudi citizen and currently a detainee a Guantanamo Bay. He's one of the last remaining detainees. We're trying to decide what to do with him. We think he still has intelligence value, so we brought him to Langley for special interrogation. That's all I'm going to tell you."

They proceeded up the stairs to an interrogation room with a one-way observation window. After they entered the guarded room, Agent Johnson introduced Zeke to Mohammed al Qahtari.

Zeke introduced himself to Mohammed. "Do you know why we're both here?" asked Zeke.

"They say you can make me talk. Good luck. I have been tortured relentlessly by your government."

"Well, I assure you that I'm not going to torture or physically harm you in any way," replied Zeke.

Zeke extended his hand in a gesture of a handshake to which Mohammed reciprocated. He looked Mohammed in the eye. Zeke saw that not only did Mohammed have no armor, but a snake-like thing coiled around him. It was similar to the creature that possessed Abdul Muti Poya. But it had only one raptor-like head that sat above Mohammed's head and hissed at Zeke.

"Who are you?" asked Zeke.

"I am Leviathan," the creature replied.

"Demon of pride?" asked Zeke.

"That I am."

"I need to talk to Mohammed," replied Zeke.

"Mohammed works for me," replied the demon.

"In the name of the Lord of Hosts, I demand to talk to Mohammed," said Zeke. Zeke commanded a greater authority in the faith than when first talked to the Legion demons.

"Why are you at Guantanamo Bay?" asked Zeke.

"They say I am terrorist," responded Mohammed.

"Are you?" asked Zeke.

"No," replied Mohammed, "I am not terrorist."

"Who are you then?"

"I am member of Al-Qaeda."

"Al-Qaeda is a terrorist group," replied Zeke.

"Al-Qaeda is not terrorist group. Al-Qaeda defends Muslim homelands from Soviets and American infidels."

"What was your involvement with Al-Qaeda?"

"I failed to execute mission," replied Mohammed.

"What was your mission?"

"Hijack airplane."

"When?" asked Zeke.

"June eleventh two thousand and seventeen," replied Mohammed.

"Why did you fail?"

"No entry U.S. No entry."

"So, you were supposed to stage the June eleventh attack, but never made it into the U.S.?" asked Zeke.

"Yes. Infidels hold me three years."

"What crime have they charged you with?" asked Zeke.

"No crime."

"So, why haven't they let you go?" asked Zeke.

"Intel, they say they need more intel from me?"

"Do you have more intel?"

"No," replied Mohammed. "I tell them all I know. No more. I have no more."

"What intel did you give them?" asked Zeke.

"The president of United States. I tell them plot on president of United States."

"What about the president?" asked Zeke. "What's going to happen to the president?"

"We kill infidel president."

"When?"

"Thank you day. We kill him on thank you day."

"You mean Thanksgiving Day?" asked Zeke.

"Yes," replied Mohammed. "Thank you day."

Zeke pulls his hand away from Mohammed who looks at him in a daze.

Agent Johnson rushed into the room. "Zeke, come with me."

Agent Johnson took him into the viewing room behind the one-way glass. There he met the former lead of the CIA's Remote Viewing Stargate Program, Mr. Cramer, Deputy Director Crenshaw of the Central Intelligence Agency, and the Director Whitehead of National Intelligence.

"Zeke, pleasure to meet you," said Deputy Director Crenshaw. "We've known of the assassination plot on the president planned for this Thanksgiving when the president is scheduled to visit the troops in Afghanistan. We've known about it for a few months. You just confirmed it for us. Son, thank you for what you've done here today in service to our country. We would like to bring you on board in a consulting capacity. You will be a part of a new program in the Directorate of Operations (DO) which is the old Clandestine

Service. They are being funded to develop new interviewing techniques on intelligence assets. We will keep you on retainer and call upon you as needed to confirm existing intelligence or gain further intelligence. Agent Johnson will continue to be your hander. Welcome to the CIA."

"Thank you, sir," replied Zeke. "Happy to serve."

"Zeke, come over here," said Agent Johnson. "I want you to meet the former trainer of our remote spies. This is Russel Garg. Mr. Garg, this is Zeke Jackson."

"Wonderful to meet you son. You definitely have a gift. I've been watching your interviews. Zeke, you definitely have a psychic gift. I would like to study it sometime."

"Sir, I'm not a psychic. My gift is not psychic in nature. It's supernatural and spiritual in nature."

"It doesn't matter to me. I don't try to differentiate," said Mr. Garg.

"It matters to me," said Zeke.

"Why?" asked Mr. Garg.

"Because I believe that psychic means demonic, and I don't want to receive anything from a demonic force."

"Oh, you're one of those people," said Mr. Garg.

"What do you mean?" said Zeke.

"You're one of those religious people who think that science is evil," said Mr. Garg.

"No, but I think that science needs to be explained within the context of God," said Zeke.

"How's that work for remote viewing?" asked Mr. Garg.

"Assuming that remote viewing is an ability of a godly, spiritual nature then its source would be godly. There are two spiritual forces in this world, God and Satan, good and evil. The big question is: from which source is your information coming?"

"Why should I care?" asked Mr. Garg.

"A demonic force lives in the spiritual realm of Satan, not God," replied Zeke. "It is anti-God. I would not exercise my gift if I thought its source was demonic in nature."

"We should talk more sometime," said Mr. Garg.

"Would love to," replied Zeke.

Then, Zeke spotted General Hartack in the room. "General Hartack, what are you doing here?" asked Zeke.

"I run one of the remote viewing programs for the Army. I was very impressed with your demonstration. Good to see you coming on board," said General Hartack.

"Thanks," said Zeke.

"General Hartack, good to see you," said Agent Johnson. "If you'll excuse us, Zeke and I need to get out of here. I need to get him the correct badge and process him through."

After Zeke and Agent Johnson left the viewing room, Agent Johnson explained Zeke's role. "Now, Zeke, you understand that you will not be an employee of the CIA, but a consultant to the CIA?"

"Yes, that's fine with me," said Zeke.

"You will be part of the Directorate of Operations. I'm a DO officer. Part of our mission is the collection of human intelligence or HUMINT and covert action. You will be used in the gathering of human intelligence. You were not put though all the rigorous physical and mental training required of the rest of the DO officers. We only intend to use you for HUMINT in a controlled environment."

"What does that mean?"

"You won't be used in the field, just in an office environment."

"You mean no jumping out of airplanes?" asked Zeke. "No car chases?"

"Afraid not," replied Agent Johnson.

"No James Bond?"

"I tell you what. After we're done here, I'll buy you a martini. But that is as close as you'll get to James Bond."

"I'll take it," said Zeke.

After they had completed Zeke's administrative processing, Agent Johnson offered to take Zeke to dinner at the Hay Adams Hotel in downtown DC. On the way, Zeke asked if he could invite Abby.

"Sure," said Agent Johnson.

Zeke called her on his cell.

"Hey, Zeke," greeted Abby.

"You'll never guess where I'm at right now."

"Where? What happened today?" asked Abby.

"Well, I'm with Agent Johnson and we're on our way to the Hay Adams Hotel in DC for dinner. Can you meet us there?"

"OK, I'll be there."

When they arrived at the hotel, they proceeded to the Lafayette Dining Room. Zeke texted Abby where to meet them. They were seated and both ordered martinis from the bar.

"Actually, this is a tradition in the DO," said Agent Johnson. "Whenever we onboard a new agent, we take them out for a martini."

"Shaken or stirred?" asked the waiter.

"Shaken, not stirred," replied Zeke.

"Zeke, I prefer that you call me Tom. I think we can be on a first name basis now. Anyway, it's less conspicuous than calling me Agent Johnson."

"Certainly. Oh, there's Abby," said Zeke who had a view of the lobby. Zeke stepped just out of the restaurant to get Abby's attention.

"Abby, over here," called Zeke.

"Hey, I got here as soon as I could. Didn't have time get to put on dinner clothes," said Abby.

"You look great," said Zeke. "Come on. We've got a table and already ordered drinks."

"Abby, good to see you," greeted Agent Johnson.

"Good to see you again, Tom. Thanks for all you've done for Zeke."

"He'll be a good asset for the agency. Do you want to join us in a celebratory martini?"

"Sure," replied Abby.

"This is a time of celebration. The meal is on me," said Tom.

"Well, in that case, I'll have the filet mignon," said Abby.

"Me too," said Zeke.

"Waiter," called Tom. "Filet mignon all around."

"I'll get the order right in, sir," replied the waiter. "And your drinks will be right out."

"So, Zeke, what are you going to do about your day job at the station?" asked Abby.

"My boss and I are supposed to talk about that. He told me to think stringer."

"What's a stringer?" asked Agent Johnson.

"A stringer is a freelance journalist that gets paid by the story."

"Zeke," said Tom. "You have my permission to 'read him in' on your role with the CIA."

"What do you mean, 'read him in'?" asked Zeke.

"Inform him. Explain to him, etc.," said Tom. "You can explain your role as a consultant and asset to the CIA using your gift. You can't tell him about the details of the assassination or what you're uncovering. You can tell him that I'm your handler. Any stories involving your work at the agency need to be vetted by me," instructed Agent Johnson.

"Got it." replied Zeke. "Thanks, that will go a long way to easing tensions with Harvey."

"Toast to Zeke and his future cooperation with the agency," said Abby. As the martini glasses clanged and their steaks arrived, the three sealed a friendship that would transcend government agencies. When they finished, Agent Johnson drove Zeke back to his car in Langley.

"Zeke, it's been a good day. Welcome to the CIA. I look forward to working with you."

"What will you do about the assassination plot on the president?" asked Zeke.

"We'll work with the Secret Service. They'll cancel his upcoming trip to Afghanistan. Then, we have to find out who is behind this. Get some rest. Go to your real job tomorrow. I'll be in touch."

"Thanks, Tom. Good night."

Zeke drove to his house in Silver Spring. Again, the day's events had been so draining that his drive home felt like he was sleepwalking around the beltway, which was not unlike the experience of many of the DC drivers, whose commutes ran anywhere from thirty minutes to four hours depending on traffic.

The next morning Zeke awoke to his alarm at 7:00 am. He showered, shaved, brushed his teeth, and went to the station. His mind was still on the day before, and he was thinking about his conversation with Harvey. Certainly, a cup of coffee and a bagel would help him come up with the right thing to say. So, he went a little out of his way to stop at a Starbucks on the way into work. After arriving at the station, he decided to use a rear entrance to bypass Harvey's eyes and ears, Julie. Zeke made his way upstairs to his cube.

"Hey, big shot," said Sly, who was sitting at his desk. "Nice of you to show up today."

"Well, it's Friday and I need to pick up my paycheck," replied Zeke with a smirk.

"Harvey wants to see you."

"Of course, he does," said Zeke.

Zeke walked into Harvey's office. "Zeke, we need to talk. Close the door."

"I know," said Zeke. "But before we begin, I'd just like to thank you for being very generous to me. I've had some time to think about all of this, and I want to thank you for all the time off for family stuff and to work things out with my government contacts. By the way, my aunt didn't die. I just needed to figure some things out."

"I'm not stupid, kid."

"I know I haven't been in the employ of the station for very long, and you've tolerated a lot. Also, I appreciate the headquarters opportunity, but that just wasn't me. The more I thought about it, the worse I felt for using this gift God gave me to expose Larry Cong in that way."

"Hey, kid, don't make this any harder for me than it needs to be."

"Oh, you're firing me?" asked Zeke.

"No, I don't fire good reporters, but this isn't fair to the rest of the staff. I can't 'just keep the paycheck coming' as you put it. Just because you have this unique gift doesn't mean you can come and go as you please even if it does give you an incredible edge on unearthing stories."

"OK. I've taken advantage. My apologies. It won't happen again," said Zeke.

"Apology accepted, but I think it would be better for both of us if you we're to terminate your employment voluntarily with WJOP. But I want you to continue as a stringer. I'll pay you the going rate for every story we air, and I'll put your submissions at the top of the list for consideration. Do we have a deal?"

"Definitely," replied Zeke. "Harvey, I want to 'read you in.'"

"Are you sure, kid? I don't want you to have to kill me."

"My handler, Agent Johnson, said it was OK." Zeke proceeded to bring Harvey up to speed about his involvement in the CIA.

"Are you helping them uncover the assassination plot?" asked Harvey.

"I can neither confirm nor deny. I've told you all that I can tell you," replied Zeke.

"Thanks for telling me, kid. I expected as much, but it's good to hear you say it."

Instead of extending his hand to Zeke, Harvey pulled out his bottle of scotch. "I think this is a scotch moment," said Harvey.

"I think I'll pass. You have one for me," said Zeke.

"I think I'll take the liberty. To you, Zeke," said Harvey as he downed a shot. "Kid, I want you and Sly to keep working on this assassination thing. Dig deeper."

Zeke went back to his desk. While eating his bagel and drinking coffee, he wrote a kind termination letter to Harvey and emailed Sly a copy.

"So, you're quitting?" asked Sly.

"Officially, yes. I won't be on the payroll, but I'll still be submitting stories as a stringer. I'll be around, stopping in from time to time. In the meantime, Harvey wants us to work on this assassination story together."

Zeke began to do some research on the protest leader, Abdul Muti Poya who Agent Johnson had been monitoring. He found out that Poya made a trip to Afghanistan as recently as two weeks ago. Zeke decided that he wanted to ask Poya some more questions, so he told Harvey and took Sly with him on another trip to the apartment of Abdul Muti Poya. This time he did not take a camera crew so as not to scare off the already skittish Poya.

Zeke and Sly took a WJOP car and proceeded down Route 1. As they passed University of Maryland, few students were on the lawn in front of the chapel and all was quiet. It was before noon. They drove a few more miles down Route 1 past the University to Riverside Apartments. Abdul Muti Poya was in Apartment 201. Zeke led the way to Abdul's apartment and knocked on the door.

Zeke called his name, "Abdul Muti Poya." He knocked again. "Abdul Muti Poya." He waited a few minutes and knocked a third time, afterward calling his name, "Abdul Muti Poya."

Finally, he answered. "What do you want?

"I want to talk to you," answered Zeke. "I was here once before."

"Who are you?"

"I'm Zeke Jackson, and this is Sly McDonald with WJOP News."

"Oh, I remember. You're the guys that brought the cops to my house."

"No, no," replied Zeke. "I brought no one but myself and my camera crew."

"Do you have a camera crew now?" asked Abdul.

"No, just my coworker, Sly."

"What do you want?"

"Just to talk," replied Zeke.

"About what?"

"About your group, the Four Point Front."

"What about them?"

"Can we come in?" asked Zeke.

Abdul opened the door slightly but hesitated to make eye contact. Zeke could see a chain still strung across the doorjamb.

After several seconds Abdul untethered the door from its lock and let them in.

"What do you want to know?" asked Abdul.

"Is your group peaceful?" asked Zeke.

"Of course. We kill nobody. We love people. We fight for their well-being."

"Do you want to overthrow the government?" asked Zeke.

"The government is corrupt. It needs to be replaced."

"We have elections for that," replied Zeke.

"Your elections are corrupt. We cannot wait that long, and we cannot rely upon them," said Abdul.

"Who funds your group?"

"The people fund the group."

"Is the group funded by Americans only?"

"Well, we do have some sympathetic colleagues in other countries."

"Abdul, thank you for letting us talk to you and represent your perspective to the public," said Zeke while extending his hand.

Abdul shook Zeke's hand. Immediately, Zeke was confronted by the demon, Legion, but it was different this time. The creature reared its three heads back in apprehension.

"What do you want?" asked Legion.

"I want to talk to Abdul," replied Zeke.

"We sense that you come in strength."

"Yes, He is with me. He indwells me," replied Zeke.

"Proceed. Do us no harm," said Legion.

"Abdul, did you recently make a trip to Afghanistan?" asked Zeke.

"Yes," replied Abdul.

"Why?"

"To get money."

"Money for what?" asked Zeke.

"Money for weapons," answered Abdul.

"Why didn't you just have them wire the money?"

"Untraceable. We need it untraceable," said Abdul.

"How did you get it through customs?" asked Zeke.

"We have our ways."

"Who? Who wanted it untraceable?" asked Zeke.

"Ronald."

"Ronald who?" asked Zeke.

"Ronald Burch."

"Who is he?"

"He is weapons man."

Zeke pulled his hand away.

Zeke noticed Abdul shaking his head and rubbing his eyes. "What happen? Did I tell you about Burch? Why do you want to know about Burch?" Abdul went over to the bay window. "The police are here again. You bring them. Both times you come, you bring them."

"No, no, I did not bring them," replied Zeke. "I assure you. They must be surveilling you. Haven't you noticed them at other times?"

"Maybe," replied Abdul. "The American government, always spying and creeping around. No privacy. They violate everything. You go now. American media, almost as bad as American government."

"I'm writing a newscast on the Four Point Front, and I'd like to mention you in the article. Can I mention you?" asked Zeke.

"Yes," said Abdul.

"Is there anything that you would like me to say?" asked Zeke.

"Say for me, 'American government, your day is coming.'"

"Thanks for your time," said Zeke, and they left.

On the way out, Zeke noticed an unmarked car. Like he figured, it was Agent Johnson, but he didn't go over to him. He did not want to raise Sly's suspicions any further.

"That's your friend, isn't it?" asked Sly.

"That's the friend you were talking with in front of the White House. What's he CIA or something?"

"Or something," said Zeke.

On the way back to the station, Zeke asked Sly not to divulge the information about Agent Johnson or the procurement to anyone, even Harvey. He had no reason to trust Sly, so he promised him that he would give him full credit when it was time to release the whole story, at least everything they could release. Sly agreed.

Once they got back, Zeke and Sly co-wrote a story on the Four Point Front led by Abdul Muti Poya. They portrayed Abdul as a protest leader and organizer angry with the government. Harvey was not particularly satisfied with the story. He thought it lacked meat, but Zeke and Sly assured him there was not much more they could dig up on Abdul at this time.

Zeke's cell phone vibrated. It was Agent Johnson. "Zeke, can you come right over to the agency? I need to talk to you face-to-face. It's important."

"OK, I'll come right over. It's Friday night, you know. It'll take me about ninety minutes and that's being optimistic," said Zeke.

"Stop complaining and just get over here."

"You got it," replied Zeke.

Zeke took his usual route. Two hours later, he was entering the CIA building. This time he at least had a badge and credentials to get in. He still called Agent Johnson from the lobby. Agent Johnson came down and the two went to one of the SCIF offices on the second floor that had been reserved. After Agent Johnson entered the combination, Zeke pushed open the door and found Abby sitting in one of the chairs.

"I don't understand. Why are you here, Abby?" asked Zeke.

"Zeke, don't worry," said Agent Johnson. "It's nothing nefarious. I wanted to talk to you two together, and this conversation is highly classified. Actually, Abby is in the dark as much as you are, Zeke. Have a seat," said Agent Johnson as he sat down himself.

"OK," said Zeke.

"What do you guys think about working together?"

"At the CIA?" asked Abby.

"Well, not exactly," said Agent Johnson.

"What I have in mind will only be temporary. I want you two to team up on investigating the assassination plot."

Zeke looked at Tom and asked, "*What*?"

Abby looked at Tom and asked, "*What*?"

"You two act like a team already," said Tom.

"I'm not an investigator," said Zeke. "You bring me people, and I'll ask them questions for you using my gift, but I'm not an investigator."

"I know that, Zeke. Don't worry. I'll tell you who to talk to."

"I may be a clearance investigator, but this is out of my league," said Abby. "Plus, my boss is not gonna like this."

"Don't worry, Abby. I'll take care of that. I'll clear it with your boss. And, as far as investigations go, you're already in the wheelhouse. You'll find this a natural progression."

Abby folded her arms and leaned back in her chair. "Ah, OK," said Abby.

Zeke scratched his head. "I don't...OK," said Zeke."

"That settles it then," said Agent Johnson. "I'll be in touch this week with further instructions. For now, you can start by searching the NCIC, IAFIS, N-Dex, and TIDE databases for whatever you can find on Abdul Muti Poya. I'll request accounts for Zeke on N-Dex and TIDE. Zeke, you probably have an account on NCIC through WJOP.

"That's right," said Zeke.

"Abby, do you need me to get you access to any of those databases?" asked Agent Johnson.

"No, I've already got access to all of them."

"Great. You two close the door on the way out and behave yourselves. I've got to get home to the wife."

"Working with you is not exactly what I had in mind," said Zeke. "I have other plans for you."

"You do, do ya?" replied Abby with a coy smile. "When were you planning on telling me about those plans?"

"Well, I was just getting ready to call you when Tom called me and told me to get over here."

"So, Zeke, what are those other plans you had in mind for me?" asked Abby.

"Well, I was thinking of which restaurant to ask you to. Then, I thought, we've never actually dated, but we're beyond just dinner. So, how about a day trip to Colonial Williamsburg, Virginia. Pre-Thanksgiving is a great time of year for Williamsburg. The only time better is pre-Christmas, but we might luck out and see some early Christmas decorations."

"I love Colonial Williamsburg," said Abby. "When did you get to be such a Washingtonian?"

"Someone at the station told me about it. Said it was a must see. How about next Saturday?"

"Sounds good," said Abby. "I'll text you my address."

"OK, I'll pick you up at eight next Saturday morning?"

The two closed the door on the way out of the SCIF. They exited the building and drove home.

The next morning, Zeke put a pot of coffee on the gas stove. He had one of those old 1950s metallic pots which he filled with water and put the grinds in a contraption that he lowered into the pot. As the coffee percolated filling the house with a wonderful aroma, he started waking up. His mind went to Ronald Burch. He got on his laptop and looked up his name in the NCIC database but nothing. He really needed to look him up in the TIDE and N-Dex databases where he could better see and correlate terrorist activities. For that he would need Abby. She had access, and he figured Agent Johnson hadn't yet requested it for him. He poured himself a cup of coffee in his Waffle House mug and called Abby.

"Abby, good morning," greeted Zeke. Hope I didn't wake you."

"It's ten o'clock. I've been up since seven," said Abby. "What's up?"

"Can you look up a suspect in your TIDE and N-Dex databases for me?"

"Did Tom call you?" asked Abby.

"No," replied Zeke.

"Well, who is this person?"

"His name is Ronald Burch," replied Zeke.

"How did you get his name?"

"I got it from Abdul Muti Poya.

"Who is Ronald Burch?" asked Abby.

"I don't really know, but Abdul said he handles weapons procurement for them. He doesn't show up in the NCIC database. I want to find out if he's on anyone's radar."

"Sure, I'll run a check on him, but then we should wait for Tom's instructions. I'll call you after I run the checks."

"OK. Thanks, Abby."

Zeke brushed his teeth, put on some old dingy jeans and got a rake out of his shed. Then he went out and began raking leaves that had dropped from the old annoying silver maple tree in his front yard. He pushed them to the curb for the city to pick up. Back home, they would just burn them and enjoy the smell, but they weren't allowed to burn anything here. Still, it was a welcomed distraction. When Zeke finished, he went inside, showered and shaved.

Late that afternoon, Abby called. "Ronald Burch is clean," said Abby.

"What? That can't be," said Zeke.

"I checked all the databases," said Abby.

"Did you check TIDE and N-Dex?" asked Zeke.

TIDE was a database of known or suspected international terrorists contributed to by the CIA, FBI, NSA, and DIA. It was the source for the FBI's terrorist database, TSDB.

N-Dex was a smart database that facilitated interagency connections correlating data among persons, places, and things.

"Yes," said Abby. "Nothing."

"This guy is working with Abdul Muti Poya, but he's not on anyone's radar?" asked Zeke.

What's Ronald Burch's deal? wondered Zeke.

"Don't worry about it. We can ask Tom when he calls. Meanwhile, what are you doing for dinner?" asked Abby.

"I'm beat. I just got done raking the leaves," said Zeke." I just want to make a sandwich and then go to bed early and get up and go to church.

By Wednesday Zeke hadn't heard from Agent Johnson, so he called Abby. "Abby, what's going on? Have you heard anything?"

"No, not a word from Tom. Something probably sprung up which totally sucked him in," said Abby. "I'm sure he hasn't forgotten about us."

"All right, later," said Zeke.

Zeke called Agent Johnson.

"Zeke, I was just going to call you and Abby. I apologize. Things have been crazy around here. Terrorist chatter has been high. Can you come over to Langley?"

"When?"

"Now," said Agent Johnson. "I'll call Abby and tell her."

"OK. See you in about an hour," said Zeke.

Zeke and Abby met in the lobby of the CIA building. Security called Agent Johnson and told him Zeke and Abby were waiting for him.

"I've reserved a SCIF upstairs. Let's go," said Agent Johnson after he entered the lobby. After they walked up to the SCIF and Agent Johnson entered the combination, all three went in. and took a seat.

"Things are starting to heat up on the Muti Poya front," said Agent Johnson. "We're starting to hear more and more overseas chatter. Poya's name has been mentioned but he hasn't actually spoken to anyone. Abby, I want you to run some queries on Abdul Muti Poya in the TIDE and N-Dex databases looking for conversations and contacts he's had in the last month. Also, any places of significance he's been in the last month."

"What are we looking for?" asked Abby.

"Anything that ties him to the presidential assassination, a possible money trail from overseas, funding from overseas," said Agent Johnson.

"Did you inform my supervisor that I'd be working on this?" asked Abby.

"I talked to him this morning," said Tom. "You're all set. I convinced him it was good for interagency relations and good experience for you. Zeke, I want you to interview Abdul again. Find out his connection to Ahmad Khan Afghan. Take Abby with you."

"Last time I interviewed him, he told me that he made a trip back to Afghanistan last month to get money from his Afghan backers for his protest efforts," said Zeke.

"Yes, we know," said Agent Johnson. "We eavesdropped on your conversation from the car."

"Then you know about Ronald Burch," said Zeke.

"He's just a local arms dealer. He doesn't have international ties. Don't worry about him," said Agent Johnson.

"Did you get me access to the TIDE and N-Dex databases?" asked Zeke.

"No, the IT people never got to it. Don't worry. Abby has access," said Agent Johnson.

"But I don't want to have to bother her all the time," replied Zeke. "Why don't you give me the names of the IT staff so I can check on it?"

"That's OK," replied Agent Johnson. "I'll take care of it."

"Tom, just an FYI," said Abby. "Zeke and I will be out of town on Saturday. We're going to Williamsburg."

"It's not a problem. Have fun. Now, you two get out of here."

"Zeke, I'm going back to my office to check through these databases," said Abby. "Call me when you want to go see Abdul."

"OK, I need to think about how to approach him," replied Zeke. "I may be wearing out my welcome."

The two left the SCIF and the building. Zeke headed back to WJOP. When he arrived at the station, he jogged up the familiar white stone steps leading to the arched entrance. Once inside, he was greeted by Julie.

"Zeke, I heard you're leaving us," said Julie.

"Not really," said Zeke. "I'll still be around, just not on the payroll as an employee."

"Where are you going?" asked Julie.

"I'm launching out on my own as a stringer. A freelancer if you will."

"Wow, that's scary," replied Julie. "I need the security of a regular paycheck."

"Well, I've got some other things in the fire. I'll be OK."

"Like what?" asked Julie.

"I can't say," said Zeke.

On his way to his desk, Zeke stopped by the coffee room where he ran into Ellie from social media.

"What's this I hear about you leaving?" asked Ellie.

"It's true I'm afraid."

"You were really tearing it up around here. I thought you might take the job at BlackRock. Everybody knew. That kind of news travels fast around here."

"That really wasn't my thing. I felt terrible about that interview with Jack Cong."

"Headquarters loved it. Ratings went through the roof," said Ellie. "Our social media just exploded."

"Maybe so, but I wonder how Jack liked it. I should call him and see how he's doing. Apologize or something."

"Well, Zeke it's not gonna be nearly as exciting without you around here."

"Hey, I'll be around. I'm gonna be a stringer for Harvey."

"Oh, that's good to hear. Good luck. See you around."

Zeke went to Harvey's office and knocked on his door.

"Come in," yelled Harvey. "Hey, kid. Wrapping up your last two weeks on the payroll?"

"I guess you could say that. I'm still working the assassination story, and I'm working some leads, but I need time for things to develop further."

"Maybe I'm too soft sometimes, but the only story I'm expecting from you is the assassination story. So, follow whatever leads you need. Go where your contacts tell you. Just get me the story. By the way, you're on the hook for this. If it's still going after your two weeks, I'm not paying any stringer fees," said Harvey.

"OK, Boss, you got it."

"And, keep Sly in the loop," said Harvey.

Zeke stopped by Sly's cubicle. "What's up, Zeke?" said Sly.

"This is a long shot but have you ever heard of a guy by the name of Ronald Burch?" asked Zeke.

"That name sounds familiar," said Sly. "But I can't place it off the top of my head. Did you look him up in NCIC?"

"Yeah, I didn't find anything. If it comes to you, let me know."

"Anything happening on the assassination front?"

"No, not really."

"Keep me in the loop, man," said Sly.

"Don't worry, I will," said Zeke.

As Zeke walked away, he called Abby from his cell. "Hey, it's five o'clock. Do you want to get some dinner?"

"Sure, I'll meet you at Harriet's in thirty minutes," said Abby.

"Better make that fifty minutes. It's rush hour," said Zeke.

"OK," said Abby.

When Zeke arrived at the restaurant, Abby was already there and had selected a table. Zeke spotted her and went to her table.

"Have you been waiting long?" asked Zeke.

"About ten minutes," said Abby. "How was traffic?"

"Not that bad. I guess I'm getting used to it."

The waitress stopped by their table.

"I'll have the unsweetened tea," said Abby.

"Same here," said Zeke.

"Are you ready for your entrée or do you need more time?" asked the waitress.

"I'm ready," said Zeke. "How about you, Abby?"

"I'll have the Atlantic salmon," said Abby.

"I'll have the meatloaf," said Zeke. The waitress left to fill the order. "Find anything in the databases?" asked Zeke.

"Yeah, plenty," said Abby. "I was able to correlate a lot of data among three databases. But I think we should wait till we talk to Tom at the Langley facility before discussing it."

"Oh, yeah," agreed Zeke. "After dinner, I'll call him and schedule a time when we can both talk to him in a SCIF."

"Sounds good," said Abby as their food appeared.

After they were done eating, Zeke called Agent Johnson.

"Agent Johnson, this is Zeke. Abby has been able to correlate some data, and we're ready to meet with you."

"Have you interviewed Poya yet?" asked Agent Johnson.

"No, we're going to see him tomorrow."

"I'll put you on my schedule for eleven o'clock Friday morning. That way you will have had a chance for a fresh talk with Poya."

"OK. See you then," said Zeke.

Zeke turned to Abby and told her about the appointment with Agent Johnson at Langley on Friday. He also told her about interviewing Abdul beforehand. "I'll meet you at Abdul's apartment in Riverside tomorrow at eleven am, Riverside Apartments, Apartment 201."

"OK, said Abby. "Have a restful night. I'll see you at Abdul's."

"Don't dress like a cop," said Zeke.

"How does a cop dress?" asked Abby.

"You know. Black slacks, white shirt, and black jacket," said Zeke.

Zeke went home but did not have a good night's sleep. He was awakened by a frightening dream of a large six-headed viper pursuing him. The next morning, he put on a pot of coffee. After pouring a cup into his comforting Waffle House mug, he sat at the kitchen table, Bible in hand, looking for a comforting passage of scripture and asking the Lord to be with him as he went up against the unknown. He was challenged by what seemed to be the familiar verse that was defining his life, Ephesians 6:12:

For we wrestle not against flesh and blood, but against principalities, against powers, against the rulers of the darkness of this world, against spiritual wickedness in high places.

But he was comforted by another verse, 2 Timothy 1:7:

For God hath not given us the spirit of fear; but of power, and of love, and of a sound mind.

After Zeke finished his coffee and praying, he showered, shaved, and brushed his teeth before getting in his truck and driving to Abdul's apartment. He met up with Abby, who was waiting for him in her car in the parking lot.

When Abby got out of the car, Zeke told her to leave her badge.

They went up to Abdul's apartment. They knocked, and Zeke spoke Abdul's full name loudly without shouting.

"Who wants to know?" answered Abdul.

"Zeke Jackson with WJOP and my partner Abby Sorensen."

"You bring cops?"

"No," said Zeke. "Check your window."

"OK. No cops," said Abdul.

The door opened slightly with a chain latch preventing it from opening fully.

“What do you want?” asked Abdul.

“Did you listen to the last WJOP story on the Four Point Front?”

“Yes,” replied Abdul.

“Did you like it?”

“Yes, I like. You say what I tell you to say.”

“Good. I’m writing another story on your group. Can I talk to you some more?”

“I guess.” Abdul unlatched the chain lock and let them in.

“I brought you a video of the story on your group for you to keep as a promo for your recruits,” said Zeke as he handed Abdul the video with his right hand. Abdul grabbed the video with his right hand, but Zeke quickly slipped the video away with his left hand and grabbed Abdul’s extended hand. “A few questions first.”

After making eye contact, he was again confronted by the snake-like thing coiling around Abdul. Its three raptor-like heads sat above Abdul’s head once again hissing at Zeke.

“Are you Legion?” asked Zeke.

“That we are,” replied the demon.

“I want to talk to Abdul.”

"What business do you have with our servant Abdul?" asked the demon.

"I come in the name of the Lord of Hosts. Move aside."

The demon sensed a strong presence of the Lord. "We will allow it. Do us no harm."

Zeke proceeded to ask his questions of Abdul. "Do you know Ahmad Khan Afghan?"

"Yes, I do," replied Abdul.

"Who is he?"

"He is my cousin," replied Abdul.

"Where is he?" asked Zeke.

"He's at the music store looking at guitars," said Abdul.

"Which store?" asked Zeke.

"Chuck Levin's Music Store in Wheaton," said Abdul.

Zeke pulled away from Abdul thanking him for the interview. He and Abby left the apartment and talked on the way to the parking lot. They agreed to meet at Chuck Levin's, off Veirs Mill Road. As they pulled into the parking lot, they spotted Ahmad getting into a car.

"Ahmad Khan," they yelled.

"Yes," he replied as he got out of the car.

"My name is Zeke Jackson with WJOP, and this is my partner Abby Sorensen," said Zeke as he extended his hand.

"We were just talking with your cousin, Abdul Muti Poya, who told us we could find you here."

Ahmad took his hand. Zeke was immediately confronted by a snake-like thing that coiled around Ahmad's six-foot-four frame. This one was much larger and had six-raptor like heads that sat above Ahmad's head and hissed at Zeke.

"Who are you?" asked Zeke.

"I am Abaddon," the creature replied.

"Angel of death?" asked Zeke.

"Yes, the destroyer, angel of the great abyss. My time is yet to come."

"What do you want with Ahmad?" asked Zeke.

"He belongs to me. He is my servant. He is on a mission," replied the creature.

"What mission," asked Zeke.

"You know," replied the creature.

"Be gone from him," commanded Zeke.

"I do not listen to you. You cannot defeat me alone."

"In the name of the Lord Jesus Christ, be gone," commanded Zeke once again.

"Leave us before we destroy you," said the angel of death.

"I am protected by the Lord of Hosts. You cannot harm me," said Zeke.

"Maybe so, but the Lord of Hosts is not going to grant your request today," replied the creature. "So we do not comply. Be gone."

Zeke backed off. He did not understand why the Lord was not permitting him to ask Ahmad any questions.

Zeke finished greeting Ahmad and said, "It was nice meeting you. Hope you enjoy your visit." Then, Zeke and Abby walked away.

"Why didn't you ask him any questions?" asked Abby.

"God would not allow it."

"But why not," asked Abby.

"I don't know. Maybe it wasn't the right time."

Friday morning Zeke awoke still wondering why he wasn't able to get past the angel of death, Abaddon, to question Ahmad. He put his coffee on the stove and opened his Bible. He asked the Holy Spirit to reveal to him what was preventing him from getting through.

Search me Lord and see if there be any crooked way in me. He thought of Sly and Harvey, and he held no unforgiveness. He even tried to make things right with both of them, and was comforted by Psalm 31:14–15:

But as for me, I trust in Thee, O Lord, I say, 'Thou art my God.' My times are in Thy hand…

Zeke smelled the wonderful coffee percolating. He poured a cup in his favorite mug and called Abby.

"Good morning," said Zeke.

"Good morning," said Abby.

"I'm going to head over to Langley in about an hour," said Zeke. "Do you want me to pick you up?"

"No, I'm at work," said Abby. "I'll meet you there."

Zeke attended to his personal hygiene, got dressed, and then drove to Langley. Rush hour was over, so the drive was not bad. He and Abby met in the parking lot and walked in together. They went through security. Agent Johnson was waiting for them in the lobby. The three of them went directly upstairs to a SCIF.

"What have you guys got for me?" asked Agent Johnson.

"Abdul Muti Poya is basically a protest leader, a rally organizer with anti-establishment sympathizers," said Abby. "He leads a group called the Four Point Front. He is an Afghani with relatives in Afghanistan and ties to the Taliban. He recently made a trip back to Afghanistan."

"What Abby says is true," said Zeke. "But he went to Afghanistan to get untraceable cash for weapons, not just to see relatives. He purchases weapons from Ronald Burch. Oh, another thing. Abdul's cousin, Ahmad Khan Afghan, is in town visiting him. I tried to interview him, but I could not break through."

"What do you mean, you couldn't break through?" asked Agent Johnson.

"He had a demon, a very powerful demon guarding him. He wouldn't let me ask Ahmad any questions. By the way, I still don't have access to the TIDE and N-Dex databases," said Zeke.

"Those databases are overrated. Don't get me wrong. Your analysis from those databases has been excellent, Abby," said Agent Johnson.

"I'd like to see some of that analysis," said Zeke.

"Don't worry about it, Zeke," said Agent Johnson. "Let Abby and I take care of that. The databases depend on what other people put into them. You can only correlate information that they contain. Zeke, your gift gives us on-the-ground, real-time information. Abby, enter this new info from Zeke in the N-Dex database. You two are a great team."

"Well, the great team is taking the day off and going to Williamsburg tomorrow," said Zeke.

"You two enjoy yourselves and stay out of trouble. I'll see you next week."

Zeke got a good night's sleep and arrived at Abby's doorstep at 8:00 am sharp, but not before picking up some coffee and donuts for the long ride.

"I think we'll take I-95 South," said Zeke, as they began their drive from Silver Spring where Abby also lived. As Zeke grasped the steering wheel, Abby slid close to him and stroked his large muscular hands. Zeke smiled at her.

“Those are from my father and baling hay in the summer,” he said.

By the time they got to I-95 South, it was already starting to back up.

“Eight thirty am on a Saturday?” said Zeke. “Don’t these people ever sleep in?”

“It’s life in the DMV,” said Abby. “I had to contend with this when I trained at Quantico. It’s coming up in about twenty miles.”

Zeke turned on the radio and tuned to WJOP. He didn’t recognize the newscaster. They aired the second-string newscasters on the weekend. Weekly morning and evening drive times were coveted, and very competitive in the radio business, especially in the DMV.

Abby looked across I-95 at the northbound traffic. “No slugs today,” she said.

“What’s a slug?” asked Zeke.

“A slug is a carpooler. It’s a Washington, DC thang. Slugs, as they are called, are wannabe carpoolers looking for a ride to predefined agency stops in DC, lining up at designated slug stops off I-95.”

Temperatures and an overcast sky confirmed a weather report of snow. White salt streaks ran across the highway, a sure sign that the state and federal roads officials were preparing for snow.

"So, Zeke, how tall are you?"

"You don't remember that from my SF-86?" quipped Zeke.

"I don't make it a point to remember my applicants' statistics," replied Abby.

"I'm six feet tall, one hundred and ninety pounds."

"You forgot to mention broad shoulders and intriguing dark blue eyes," complimented Abby.

"Now I know that's not on the SF-86," said Zeke.

Abby snuggled up to Zeke and ran her index finger down his nose.

"You'll do quite nicely." Abby chuckled as she gave him a peck on the cheek.

"So, what's this Christian thing all about?" asked Abby.

"Well, I was raised in the church," said Zeke, "the Pentecostal church."

"Is that the name of the church?" asked Abby.

"No, that refers to the type of church."

"Oh, you mean denomination."

"No, it's not really a denomination. There are like two hundred Pentecostal denominations."

"What do they believe?"

"They believe that Jesus Christ is the Son of God and in the Trinity and in the Bible. They are very evangelical. The big thing about the Pentecostal religion is that they are really big on promoting the gifts of the Holy Spirit, especially speaking in tongues and performing miracles and healing the sick. But that's the church I grew up in. I'm not so convinced of all that now. I mean that I'm not convinced of the tongues and miracles and healings. I think those were gifts given to the apostles for the time of the early church as a sign that Christ had risen from the dead and His church was real. I believe in all the rest of it, though. But religion is not the important thing. Religion cannot save you. Neither can tongues or healing the sick or miracles. What's important is that you repent and believe in Christ who is the Son of God."

"But why do we need to repent?" asked Abby.

"Without repentance, we are at odds with God. We have all sinned. Christ is the only sinless one. When we repent and believe, Christ becomes the propitiation for our sin. We are forgiven and reconciled to God. That is what I believe and that is what I've done."

"Wow," said Abby. "I just went to church and tried to be a good person. I didn't know I had to do all that."

The drive down I-95 toward Richmond would lull a driver to sleep if not punctuated by feelings of terror as they go from eighty miles per hour to five miles per hour.

"Hey, we're passing Quantico," said Abby. "I learned to drive there during my Basic Field Training Course."

"Well, I learned to drive in drivers ed after school," replied Zeke.

"That's not driving," said Abby. "That's just high schoolers getting their license. I completed the TEVOC course at Quantico."

"What's that?" asked Zeke.

"That's a course in how to safely catch criminals and terrorists in high speed chases."

Zeke knew Abby was an FBI Agent, but he thought she had just been a nosy office clerk who made her way into clearance investigations. He never thought of her as a real agent.

Suddenly, they heard screeching tires, a loud *bam*, the sound of crashing metal, and felt a heavy jolt as they were pushed forward. Zeke had left enough of a cushion between him and the next car so that he avoided plowing into it. The air bags had not deployed.

"Are you OK?" he asked.

"Yes," she replied. Neither of them had been injured. Zeke began to get out of the car when Abby reached over to pull him back in.

"No, Zeke," she shouted. "I don't think that was an accident."

A man got out of the car and started walking toward the driver side of Zeke's truck. He was tall and Middle Eastern.

"He's got a gun," shouted Abby. "Let me drive."

Zeke unbuckled his seatbelt and maneuvered into the back seat. Abby slid over into the driver's seat. She rotated the steering wheel to the left and punched the accelerator pulling the truck from the left lane onto the left shoulder barely missing the driver approaching on foot. Fortunately, the other driver's car was too damaged for him to pursue them. She sped down the shoulder for three or four miles until she approached a Virginia State Trooper along the side of the road. She waited for the officer to approach the car.

"What do you think you're doing?" asked Officer Jenkins. "Driver's license and registration, please."

Abby gave him her license and then reached into the glove compartment for the registration. After she gave him the registration, she pulled out her badge and showed it to him.

"FBI," said the officer.

Abby proceeded to explain to the officer that someone had been following them and then purposely rear-ended them. Then, the driver approached their truck with an unconcealed gun.

"Virginia is an open-carry state," said the officer.

"Yes, I know," said Abby.

"Where did it happen?" asked Officer Jenkins.

"About four miles back," replied Abby.

"Are you guys OK?"

"Yes," said Zeke.

"I'm writing a report," said Jenkins. "After you leave me your cell numbers and home addresses on that, you can go. If you want any additional information on the case, just call the number on the report."

"Thanks," said Zeke.

Zeke got out of the truck and checked it for damage. There was only a little bit on the bumper. It sounded a lot worse. He got back in the truck on the passenger side. After Officer Jenkins handed Abby his report, they pulled ahead and merged into the line of traffic heading to Richmond.

As Zeke and Abby continued down the road, Zeke blurted out, "And I thought you were just a clerk."

"So, only men can be real FBI agents?" asked Abby.

"No, no, that's not what I meant," said Zeke.

"Why, Joseph Black, I didn't take you for a male chauvinist."

Zeke shook his head and squeezed his eyes. Only his parents, relatives and friends back home called him that.

They finally hit the I-95/I-295 split. They took I-295 South around Richmond. It had started to snow lightly.

"Careful, Abby. This truck doesn't handle all that well in snow."

"That's Agent Sorensen to you," she said playfully.

"And you can call me Joseph. I like it when you call me Joseph."

"Really?" she said. "I thought it would remind you of a part of your past that you would rather forget."

"The high school bomb scare was a single incident. I'm not proud of it, but my childhood was so much more than that. I like where I came from. I like who I've become. I like who I am," said Zeke.

Abby took her eyes off the road for a moment, blew Zeke a kiss, and then smiled.

They took I-295 South towards Rocky Mount, North Carolina which completed the eighty-five-mile trip to Richmond. They exited I-295 South onto I-64 East, a fifteen-mile stretch of road not nearly as crowded as I-95 South. Except for the occasional trooper, they could cruise along at a comfortable seventy mph even in a light snow. A temperate wind carried the snow to the pines lining both sides of the highway. Some of it made it to the road.

The fifteen mile stretch on I-64 East soon gave way to the last leg of the trip of thirty-eight miles on US-60.

After Abby and Zeke arrived at the Colonial Williamsburg Visitor Center, they parked and went in. Abby visited the gift shop while Zeke stopped at the Information Desk where he mapped out their plan for the rest of the day. Then, he went over to the ticket window where he noticed an evening Christmas tour at Busch Gardens. The Visitor Center ran specials for tourists to Busch Gardens. This time of year, Busch Gardens had a Christmas show that started before Thanksgiving and ran most of December. Zeke thought he would be remiss if he didn't get tickets to this, and he thought Abby would like it. Afterward, he met Abby in the gift shop.

"We better get going," said Zeke. It was twelve noon, and Zeke had a full day planned. "We're going to walk over to Colonial Park. It's about half a mile."

"Can we get something to eat?" asked Abby.

"Certainly," said Zeke. "There's a couple of colonial-era restaurants in Colonial Park that I think you'll find enchanting. Can you wait?"

"Sure," said Abby. "Lead the way."

They both had dressed in light coats, jeans, and sneakers which would be quite suitable for a day of walking. But they hadn't figured on the snow which was lightly falling from the overcast sky.

They started over the bridge that led to the park along the partially paved trail. There were a few colonial placards that they stopped to read. It was colder than Zeke had anticipated, and he noticed that Abby was shivering. He offered to warm her up. She agreed. He took his light jacket and wrapped it around her. Then, he began rubbing her arms vigorously and finally pulled her close to him and held her until she stopped shivering.

"Feel better?" Zeke inquired.

"Yes, I do," replied Abby. "Thank you."

They decided to continue the journey with a slow jog to stay warm. They came off the trail and made a left onto North England Street. They continued to jog to Nicholson Street past the Market Square. When they arrived at the courthouse, Zeke asked a one of the villagers dressed in colonial garb how to get to Duke of Gloucester Street.

"You're on it," she said in plain English. He had expected some sort of Old English, thee's and thou's.

"Where is the King's Arms Tavern?" inquired Zeke.

"At the end of Gloucester on the right," said the maid. "But it's closed today. The Shields Tavern is open and is next to it." Still, no accent.

Zeke and Abby walked down thc right side of Duke of Gloucester Street until they arrived at the Shield's Tavern. The maître d' dressed in colonial garb and standing on the front steps inquired whether they would be dining for lunch. Finally, a little colonial lingo.

"Yes," said Zeke.

The maître d' ushered them into the restaurant and seated them. The menu was not that impressive, but at least they could say they ate lunch in Old Colonial Williamsburg. Zeke ordered the pulled pork sandwich with the greasy fries and Diet Coke.

"Not much selection," said Zeke.

Abby, showing a higher level of discipline, ordered the tomato basil soup and water. "You know, Zeke, there is no rule which says you have to order an entrée."

"I know," said Zeke, "but I always feel like I owe them and myself a meal."

Zeke noticed the two black waiters, one male one female, dressed in colonial garb and serving the room of white customers. Maybe it was the unsophisticated Nebraska Cornhusker in him, but he could not help but wonder if they resented the stereotypical situation in which they found themselves. A generous tip would expunge any residual white guilt, despite the sub-par cuisine.

When they finished eating, they walked back up Duke of Gloucester Street. Hearing a clop-clop-clop, they turned to see two horses pulling an old enclosed coach manned by a properly dressed driver. The snow lightly falling, the chilly air, the fresh smell of pine joined with the colonial shops to hold a close-out sale on fall.

"Let's go. We need to hurry," said Zeke.

"Why?" asked Abby.

"You'll see."

The two went into their slow jog back to the visitor center. Zeke noticed a few more horse-drawn buggies. In the distance, Zeke observed a single horse pulling a buggy.

"Look over there. That horse is trotting."

"It looks very elegant," replied Abby.

"Trotting is the most natural gait for a standard-bred horse," said Zeke. "You can always tell a trotter. It's not just the elegant look. If you watch their legs, you'll see the front and back diagonal legs moving in the same direction at the same time. The diagonal legs are in sync with each other. That's called trotting. It's called a four-beat gait, as opposed to a two-beat gait which is a pacer. Some standard-bred horses are pacers. The legs on the same side move in the same direction at the same time. This produces a side to side motion which good sulky drivers take advantage of in a race by rocking the sulky cart side to side."

"How do you know so much about this?" asked Abby.

"My grandad was a blacksmith who shoed horses. He used to take me to the races to watch the standard-bred trotters and pacers. He would hang out at the track. If a horse threw a shoe, Grandad was there to replace it."

Zeke and Abby got back to the visitor's center by about 4:30 in the afternoon. Zeke had planned to take Abby to the Christmas show at Busch Gardens a few miles up the road. By the time they got to Busch Gardens, it was about 5:00

pm and already getting dark. The darkness boded well for the Christmas lights which were out in full color.

"I love the evergreens with the white lights," commented Abby.

"I like the blue lights," said Zeke.

After they got into the park, they decided to take the gondola around the park. They waited in line until they were able to board. The gondola dropped them off in the park's Germany exhibition. They strolled around the park for about thirty minutes hoping to see some authentic Christmas shops or unique Christmas shows. Zeke noticed the disappointment in Abby's demeanor.

"You don't like it?" asked Zeke.

"I've been here in the summer," said Abby. "It seems like they just put a Christmas façade over the park and called it Christmas Town. At first, the different colored Christmas lights make it seem exciting, but after a while they grow empty and meaningless. They're just colored lights.

Finally, Zeke spotted the show, *Gloria*, and they got in line. They went to the 6:00 pm performance. The show had an orchestra pit with an entire Christmas orchestra: an organ, violins, French horns, percussion, and woodwinds. The show created a worshipful, Christmas spirit in the hearts of the audience. When they came out of the show, they talked as they made the long walk toward the entrance of the park.

Zeke knew that Abby was not enamored with the park, but he thought she enjoyed the *Gloria* show.

Before leaving the park, they stopped in a Christmas shop for some hot chocolate. Once served, they sat at one of the sidewalk tables. There, they overheard an old man at the next table reciting his unusual rendition of Psalm 23 as he watched the groups of children with their parents and the young lovers walk by observing the lights and festivities of the Christmas season.

The old man recited: "The Lord is not my shepherd. All I do is want. There are no green pastures; He leads me nowhere. He restores nothing. He guides me nowhere. When I walk through the valley of the shadow of death, I fear everything because he does not exist. Thy rod and Thy staff, they do not comfort me. Thou preparest nothing for me. Thou hast anointed my head with nothing. Surely hopelessness and despair will follow me all the days of my life, and I will dwell nowhere forever."

"Oh," said Zeke. "That's so sad. He's reciting his own version of Psalm 23."

"What?" asked Abby.

"The man at the table next to us is looking for hope in the trappings of Christmas, and he concludes his quest with his perverted version of Psalm 23."

Zeke bowed his head and began to pray quietly.

"What are you doing?" asked Abby.

"I'm praying for him, that he would believe in the Christ of Christmas, in the King of Kings, and find peace. You know, we're not kids anymore," said Zeke.

"What do you mean?" asked Abby.

"All the lights, they would have been enough. They would have been enough when I was a child," said Zeke. "But, without the real Christ, they're just empty, iconoclastic symbols of Christmas. One Christmas, when I was a kid, I looked at a ceramic Santa Claus that my mom was putting away after the holidays. I looked and looked half expecting to hear a hearty laugh or see a twinkle in his eye. But all I saw was the ceramic shell. Then, I realized that it was just a trinket of Christmas to be pulled out and put away with the arrival and departure of the season. It was the King of Kings who gave it meaning. It sounds childish, I know."

Abby leaned across the table and stared into Zeke's dark blue eyes. "It's not childish," she said. Zeke leaned in and stared into her baby blues. Their noses touched, their eyes closed, and finally their lips met in a passionate kiss.

After a few minutes they got up from the table and resumed their walk to the park's entrance. Abby reached out and took Zeke's hand, leaned into his body, and laid her head upon his shoulder as they walked.

When they got back to the entrance, they caught the tram to the parking area. They got in Zeke's truck, and he drove.

Abby slid over by Zeke, snuggled up and fell asleep the rest of the ride home.

They arrived at Abby's house at 11:00 pm. Zeke had to wake her to walk her to the door. He held her in his arms on the doorstep as they stared into one another's eyes. After one last kiss, Abby slowly left his arms, the palm of her right hand lingering on the palm of his left hand in a wistful good night.

10

Sunday Morning

The next morning, Zeke woke at 5:00 am to the sound of his phone ringing. It was the Sunday before Thanksgiving. He recognized the number on his cell. It was Agent Johnson.

"Zeke," said Agent Johnson. "Something has changed. I can't talk much over the phone. I'm sending a car to pick you up and bring you to Langley. It'll be there in thirty minutes."

"I'll be ready," replied Zeke.

Zeke got dressed, brushed his teeth, and ate a yogurt while waiting for the car. Zeke kept looking at his front window. When he saw a black suburban pull up, he went out to meet it. He was greeted by Agent Johnson in the back seat.

"Zeke, get in," said Agent Johnson, who handed him a cup of coffee in a to-go cup. "One cream, no sugar, right?"

"Yes, thanks."

There were two other men in the vehicle besides the driver. "Zeke, this is Secret Service Agent White. You've already met Secret Service Agent LaDividico."

After Zeke got in, the suburban sped away with a Secret Service escort.

"By the way," said Agent Johnson, "wait for us to knock on your door next time. You don't know who could be in the vehicle. Zeke, we have Abdul Muti Poya in custody. CIA and Secret Service brought him in. As you know, we've been surveilling him for several weeks now. Yesterday, he broke silence with his handlers. We discovered that the assassination plot originally scheduled for Thanksgiving has been moved up. We don't know exactly when or where it will take place. We want you to interview him. We want you to find out when and where the plot will go down. Can you handle it?"

"Yes," said Zeke. "I got ya covered. I'll find out when and where."

"Son," said Agent Johnson. "You pull this off and I'll make sure the president pins a medal on you."

"No medals," said Zeke. "A greet and a handshake would be appreciated, though."

They pulled into Langley at 7:00 am. The parking lot was half full. Agent Johnson and the two Secret Service agents rushed Zeke up to the second floor. They directed him into an interrogation room.

"We'll bring Abdul in shortly," said Agent Johnson. "As usual, we'll be listening, recording, and viewing from behind the glass."

As Zeke sat waiting, he contemplated his approach. The agency wanted to put Abdul on a polygraph machine and have a qualified polygrapher operating the machine while Zeke was questioning him, but Agent Johnson talked them out of it. He thought it would spook Abdul out of answering and defeat the purpose of having Zeke there in the first place. Zeke did not think it would make any difference. After all, his gift was divine in nature, not to be affected by a man-made polygraph machine. But Agent Johnson did not want to take that chance.

Agent Johnson escorted Abdul into the interrogation room and removed his handcuffs. Zeke and two armed guards were in the room.

"Hey!" said Abdul. What are you doing here?"

"That's a long story," said Zeke. "They think I might know something about you since I've been covering you and your group for the last month. They've been monitoring your apartment for a couple of months now. Let's just have some chit-chat, and I think they'll let us go when they figure out that I don't know anything more than I reported on."

Zeke extended his hand to Abdul in a gesture of friendship. Abdul reluctantly reciprocated. After locking hands, the two made eye contact.

Abdul tried to retract his hand but could not. "Let me go," cried Abdul.

"After I ask you some questions," said Zeke.

Abdul struggled, but one of the guards grabbed Abdul's shoulders forcing him into the chair while the other guard held his arm in an extended position.

"That's not necessary," said Zeke. "He can't get free until I release him. This power is not physical."

The guards insisted and continued to restrain Abdul.

Then, Zeke was confronted by the demon, Legion. The creature coiled around Abdul's body as it had before. It reared its three viper-like heads back and hissed at Zeke.

"What do you want?" asked Legion.

"I want to talk to Abdul," replied Zeke.

"We indwell him. Abdul serves us."

"The Holy Spirit indwells me," replied Zeke.

"You may proceed. Do us no harm," said Legion.

"Tell me, Abdul, have you been in contact with Mohammed al Qahtari?"

"Yes," replied Abdul.

"Was Mohammed al Qahtari involved in the Thanksgiving assassination plot of the president?"

Abdul stammered trying to prevent himself from responding. "N…n…n…n…ah. Yes," replied Abdul.

"Was that plot changed?

Again, he stammered. "N…n…n…n…ah. Yes," replied Abdul.

"What was changed?"

"I don't know," he replied.

"Was it the place and time?" asked Zeke.

"N… n…n…n…ah. Yes," replied Abdul.

"What is the new place and time?"

Abdul struggled trying to break free but could not. Then, he spurted out something they could barely understand.

"Did he say Tyson?" asked Zeke.

"That's what it sounded like to me," said a guard.

"Tyson what?" asked Zeke, tightening his grip on Abdul. "Tyson Foods?"

"At the corner," stammered Abdul.

"Tyson at the corner," said Zeke.

"Tyson's Corner," said a guard. "The place is Tyson's Corner."

"Where at Tyson's Corner?" asked Zeke.

"Church," stammered Abdul.

"When?" demanded Zeke as he gripped even tighter.

"Today," stammered Abdul.

Agent Johnson's voice boomed over the intercom. "Zeke, we got it. We figured it out. It's Tyson's Corner Bible Church at this morning's ten am service. The vice president attends this church regularly, and today he is taking the president with him. The Secret Service and FBI have been notified. The CIA along with the Secret Service and FBI will go to the church to apprehend the assassins, but the president will not be there. The president and vice president will just have to miss church today."

11

Meet Up at the Church

Agent Johnson called Zeke into the observation room filled with Secret Service, CIA, and FBI staff.

"Wow," said Zeke. "I had no idea all these people were watching.

"We didn't want to scare you," said Agent Johnson. "You impressed a lot of people today at the Agency and in the Secret Service. I'm proud of you, Zeke. We all are. But we're the silent service. We risk our lives and few people know about it. So, don't expect to see your name in the newspaper."

"That's fine with me," said Zeke, "but can you let me get a jump on the story for WJOP? I promised my boss that, whenever possible, he'd be the first to know on a good news story."

"Sure, Zeke," said Agent Johnson. "Just run it by me first."

"No problem," said Zeke.

"By the way, the CIA Director said he would arrange a meeting with the president and vice president. We're sure that when they find out what you did, they will seriously want to meet you. But the press will not know."

Agent LaDividico made his way to a black suburban vehicle. There was one other plainclothes agent in the suburban in addition to Agent LaDividico. He carried a P229 handgun chambered in a .357 SIG caliber. Agent LaDividico, who was driving, also carried the same. There were two uniformed Secret Service Agents armed with Heckler Koch MP5A3 9 millimeter machine guns.

"OK, gentlemen, listen to me," said Agent LaDividico. "We're taking the Tyson's exit. We'll be at the church in about five minutes. The parking lot is in the front of the church building. We'll park four blocks away so as not to alert the enemy. The church has a security detail, and I've phoned ahead to let them know we're coming. State police and local police have been informed and are on alert but not on the premises. I have asked them to maintain their distance. I'll signal them when to move in.

"From Zeke's interview with Poya, we know there will only be two enemy combatants including the assassin. The enemy wants this to be a surgical, precision strike, in and out. Intel tells us that they don't want to draw attention to themselves. We have no reason to believe that they are going to explode a bomb or do anything that would draw attention to themselves. Our primary concern here is that no harm comes to the congregation. I've asked the church staff to conduct their ten am service normally and they've agreed. When the enemy figures out that the president and vice president have not shown up, they will make their way out of the building. When they get outside, that's when we'll take them down."

They arrived four blocks away from the church and jumped out of the vehicle.

"Let's go. On my six. Double time to the parking lot," said Agent LaDividico. "Agent White, you bring up the rear and keep your eyes scouring the area for any enemy getaway vehicles.

"There's a man in a black car looking very suspicious," radioed Agent White ahead to Agent LaDividico. "I think that's the getaway car. I don't think he's spotted us yet."

"Take him down. We can't risk him radioing the assassins," said LaDividico.

White approached the car from the driver's side, his gun drawn. "Hands where I can see them, and don't touch that radio. Get out of the car slowly," shouted Agent White. Agent White handcuffed him.

Agent White radioed Agent LaDividico. "I got him.

"Good work", said Agent LaDividico. "I'll radio FBI to detain him, so you can continue to assist us."

When the FBI arrived, White put the combatant in the back seat of their car and they drove away.

By this time, Agent LaDividico and the two uniformed agents arrived at the church. They remained outside. There were three entrances to the church, a front, back and side entrance. The two uniformed agents with their 9-millimeter automatic machine guns manned the back and side entrances.

Agent LaDividico waited at the front entrance for White to show up. When he arrived, Agent LaDividico instructed White to man the front entrance while he went inside to search for the assassins.

Agent LaDividico entered the church from the front entrance ever so quietly, gun concealed. The church sanctuary was full of people. Two men, probably church security, stayed back in the narthex. They were armed with concealed carry. Agent LaDividico approached them and showed them his badge whispering, "Secret Service. Have you seen anything or anyone suspicious?"

"There is a man up in the choir loft," said one of the church security men. "No one else is there. He's hiding behind the organ up there. There's also a man standing at the back inside the sanctuary on the right side facing the altar. We think both men are armed. We have not approached either of them."

"Thanks", said Agent LaDividico. "You've both done good. Real good. Now, we need you men to stand down and let us take it from here."

"Yes, sir," said the men.

"But I do want you to do one more thing for me. Can I have a bulletin?" They handed him a bulletin, and Agent LaDividico began to write a note to the pastor who was engaged in his sermon at the pulpit. "I want one of you to casually walk to the front of the church and hand this note to the pastor."

The note read, "Brethren, we had expected to be graced by the presence of our president and vice president this morning, but I just learned that they will not be coming. Perhaps, they will come another time."

"Go, go now," said Agent LaDividico.

One of the men gently opened the sanctuary door, held it from making any sound as it closed and then proceeded slowly down the main aisle. He stopped in front of the pulpit and reached his outstretched arm up to the pastor with the bulletin in hand. The pastor reached down to receive it. He looked at the note, smiled and slowly raised his head toward the congregation. Then, he read the note verbatim. When he was done, he quipped," You can't believe anything politicians say." The congregation laughed and he continued with his sermon.

The man who delivered the message walked back out into the narthex.

"Did you see anything?" asked Agent LaDividico.

"Yes, the man at the back of the church was on a small radio."

"He must've been talking to the shooter," said Agent LaDividico. "Let's get out of this narthex now."

Agent LaDividico escorted the two security men out the front entrance of the church into the parking lot. After about five minutes the man at the back of the sanctuary, came out the front of the church.

Agent White, with his gun drawn, yelled "Freeze, hands in the air."

The man raised his hands and Agent LaDividico frisked him, pulling a concealed handgun from under his coat. Agent White cuffed him and Agent LaDividico took him to an unmarked FBI vehicle in the parking lot. After about five more minutes a young, tall Middle Eastern man came strolling out of the front entrance not suspecting anything and trying to look inconspicuous.

Agent White, again yelled, "Freeze, hands in the air." The man raised his hands and Agent LaDividico frisked him, but he was unarmed.

Agent LaDividico rushed up. "Are there any more of you in there?"

"You think I tell you, infidel? I am unarmed. You have nothing."

"Why does a Muslim go into a Christian church on a Sunday morning?" asked Agent LaDividico.

"I want to become Christian," said the assassin.

"Well, you're going to have to do it from behind bars."

Agent LaDividico radioed the FBI to move in as well as the state and local police. Before the incident was over, there were more law enforcement officers in the church parking lot than parishioners. The pastor dismissed the congregation telling them to leave the church building due to an incident that would be explained later. The congregation poured out into the parking lot. Many of them were going up to the local police and asking them questions.

Agent LaDividico and his agents went inside the church and began searching for weapons, bombs, and possible accomplices. The FBI followed and assisted in the search. Agent White went upstairs to the choir loft. He began looking around the loft. He found a closet, opened the door, and searched it.

"I found it! I found it!" he yelled.

"What? What did you find?" asked Agent LaDividico.

"The rifle. The rifle the assassin was going to use." Agent LaDividico ran up to the choir loft.

"Don't touch it," said Agent LaDividico. "We need to preserve any fingerprints. It looks like a Steyr SSG 69. Good choice. Most popular sniper rifle in the world. Accurate, reliable, lightweight. If you're gonna kill a president, that's the way to do it."

"You sound like you were rooting for the guy," said Agent White.

"The only thing the assassin and I have in common is that we both like guns," said Agent LaDividico.

When they had secured the building, they de-briefed the pastor and his staff. Then, they drove back to Langley.

When they got back to Langley, Zeke and Agent Johnson were waiting for them in the lobby. Agent LaDividico briefed them both on what went down at the church.

"Good work, guys," said Agent Johnson. He drove Zeke back to his home in Silver Spring.

"Well, I guess I better go into the station tomorrow," said Zeke. "I still owe Harvey a story."

"Just remember to vet it by me," reminded Agent Johnson.

"Definitely. I'll email you the story on a secure connection."

"Sounds good."

Zeke walked up to his modest three-bedroom house. The pumpkin he had placed on the front step was still sitting there surprisingly undisturbed. It wasn't the best of neighborhoods.

Time to decorate for Christmas, he thought.

Back home, his mom and dad would've already gotten a tree. They usually had one up before the end of Thanksgiving weekend.

Abby would love it there, he thought. *Nope, better squelch that. Too soon. Enough of this.*

He needed to write a story, vet it by Agent Johnson, and pitch it to Harvey. Zeke worked through the night until he finished the story and passed out on the couch. He woke up at 7:00 am to sunlight shining brightly through the living room window. Coffee...coffee...coffee...coffee...was all that ran through his brain. So, he put on a full pot and waited for it to boil. He was not sure if it was the best coffee, but the best part of coffee drinking is the smell, and that pot percolating over a gas flame filled the house with the most amazing smell that yelled, *wake up*!

He poured his first cup into a solid white coffee mug he purchased from Waffle House. No other way to drink it. So eager to taste the full-bodied aroma, he didn't even put in his usual one creamer. As he sat at the kitchen table and sipped from his first cup of the day, he realized: It was Monday morning.

Today, he would go to the station and unwrap a story that no one else had, and the world was waiting for it.

Zeke put the rest of the coffee in a thermos and took it to work with him. He pulled up to the station in his red Toyota pickup. He walked to the back of his truck and looked at his damaged bumper. He had to take care of that. It reminded him of Abby and the crazy weekend. Then, he jogged up those familiar white stone steps. There was Julie, as usual. She was a fixture at this place. Would she ever get out?

"Is this your last week?" asked Julie.

"Yep, just wrapping up a story for Harvey," said Zeke.

Zeke bounced up the stairs to the second floor. He walked up to Harvey's office and knocked on the door. "It's Zeke. Can I talk to you?"

"Come in. Are you still on the payroll?" asked Harvey.

"Last week, and I got a story for you?"

"Are you're talkin' about the assassination attempt?"

"Yep," said Zeke.

"Well, it's about time," said Harvey.

He filled Harvey in on the whole story.

"Write it up.

"I already have," said Zeke. "Of course, I can't tell the public all that I've told you, and I'll have to vet it with Agent Johnson, but I'll include whatever they allow."

"No problem," said Harvey. "Give me what you can. Let me know when Agent Johnson has approved it. We'll do a *Breaking News* piece. But I'd like to go with it no later than the Six O'clock News cycle. BlackRock is not gonna believe this."

Zeke went back to the bullpen looking for Sly, but he hadn't arrived yet. Zeke was reading over the story when Sly walked in.

"Zeke, I need to talk to you," said Sly. "I've been trying to call you, but you didn't answer."

Zeke pulled out his cell phone. His battery had died. "What is it?"

"I found Ronald Burch and paid him a visit," said Sly.

"The local weapons dealer. Agent Johnson said not to worry about him. He's legit. Abby ran him through the database and said he's clean."

"He knows Agent Johnson," said Sly.

"I'm sure Agent Johnson had reason to check him out on occasion," said Zeke.

"He did a little more than check him out," said Sly. "Agent Johnson introduced him to Abdul Muti Poya."

Zeke scratched his head. "Abdul Muti Poya and Agent Johnson are not exactly on friendly terms," said Zeke.

"Don't be so sure," said Sly.

Zeke put his hand on his head and lightly squeezed his forehead. "Wait a minute. Wai—wai—ahhhh minute. Are you suggesting that Agent Johnson has more than a legitimate connection with Abdul?"

"That's what I suspect," said Sly.

"But why would Burch admit anything to you?"

"I don't think he realized what was going on. He didn't really admit anything. I was asking him if he knew Abdul

Muti Poya, and he said yes. I asked him if he knew Agent Johnson. He said yes. He told me that Poya and Johnson came into his shop together and Johnson asked him 'to hook him up with what he needed.' That's how he put it."

"I need to talk to Agent Johnson," said Zeke. "I can't believe he has anything to do with Poya."

Zeke stopped by Harvey's office to tell him that the story was still developing and that he needed to go over to Langley to see Agent Johnson in person.

Zeke drove over to Langley without calling Agent Johnson first. On the way, he kept squeezing his nose between the index finger and thumb of his right hand.

This can't be. It really can't be, he thought. *A career CIA agent. There must be an explanation.*

Zeke arrived and entered the building. He approached security and asked them to notify Agent Johnson of a visitor.

Agent Johnson came down the stairs. "Hey, Zeke. What's up?"

"Can we take a walk outside the building?" asked Zeke.

With a look of suspicion, Agent Johnson asked, "Can't we talk here?"

"It's personal," said Zeke. "I need your advice."

"Sure," said Agent Johnson.

Zeke walked Agent Johnson to his truck.

"Get in," said Zeke.

"Where are we going?" asked Agent Johnson.

"The walking and biking path along the Potomac," replied Zeke.

After Zeke drove to the path, they got out and began walking.

"You've been like a big brother to me," said Zeke. "You took a chance on me. You instructed me, coached me, and encouraged me. You brought me on board. I owe you a lot." Zeke turned to him and offered his hand. Agent Johnson accepted it. Zeke looked him in the eye.

"What do you see?" asked Agent Johnson.

Zeke's eyes teared up. After he gained his composure, he said, "You have no armor with which to wage war against the evil one. Did you help Abdul Muti Poya secure weapons for the assassination attempt?"

"Yes," replied Agent Johnson.

"Did you tell Abdul that the president and vice president would go to that church on Sunday?" asked Zeke.

"Yes," replied Agent Johnson. "I hated him, the president. I hated his policies and what he stood for. He's such an arrogant man. He wasn't fit to be president. It's not just me, and it's not just this agency."

Special Agent LaDividico appeared from behind a tree. "We got it. Tom, I'm sorry I have to do this. I truly am," said Agent LaDividico. He cuffed him and read him his rights.

"Better you than me," said Zeke to Agent LaDividico. "I couldn't have done it."

Zeke went back to the station to finish the story. He called Special Agent LaDividico. "Agent LaDividico, Zeke here. I need you to vet this story for me. Can I send it to you?"

"Sure," said Agent LaDividico.

Zeke emailed him the story and told him he needed his feedback within the hour. When he got Agent LaDividico's feedback, he made a few quick changes and took the story to Harvey. Harvey read the first line out loud.

"On Sunday morning, the president and vice president of the United States missed church through no fault of their own."

The story ended with a comment from the pastor of Tyson's Baptist Church. He told Secret Service Agent LaDividico to tell the president and vice president that if they could not make it to church, he would gladly bring church to the White House. There was nothing incriminating about Agent Johnson or the CIA in the story.

"Good story," said Harvey. "A little bit of a soft touch, but I like it. Let Sly read it and edit it, and I'll air at six o' clock."

Zeke told Harvey about Agent Johnson and the CIA connection. But they both agreed that while the CIA revelation was a great find and would be a total bombshell, they could not go public with it at this time. There was not enough corroborating evidence for such an accusation.

"Sure thing, Boss." Zeke took the story to Sly. "Boss wants you to read and edit this. Sly, put your name on it," said Zeke. "Make sure the anchor gives you the byline. I promised you I'd give you credit for the story. Anyway, you helped me." Then he bolted out of the room to call Abby.

"Hi, Zeke. What's up?" greeted Abby.

"Hi, Abby. Could we get together and talk?"

"OK," said Abby. "Where do you want to meet?"

"How about the Pentagon Row Outdoor Ice Rink at five pm?"

"Oh, I like that place. I need to warn you, though. I'm not a very good skater."

"Don't worry. I'll help you," replied Zeke.

"OK. I'll meet you there at five pm."

It was a thirty-minute drive, but since some of the roads were closed between 3:45 and 6:30, he needed to leave at 3:30 to get past the blockages. He took Georgia Ave. South into DC and was able to beat all the road closings and get onto the Arlington Memorial Bridge crossing into Virginia by 3:45. From there he continued on Memorial Circle and took the South Arlington Boulevard Exit. He continued on South Washington Boulevard and merged onto Columbia Pike. He made a left on South Joyce Street. The Pentagon Row Outdoor Ice Rink was on his right.

The rink was surrounded by three- or four-story buildings, mostly shops but some condos. At one end of the rink stood a large Christmas tree fully decorated. At the other end were several chairs around a firepit. It was only 4 pm and still light out.

This place will turn romantic in the dark under the lights, thought Zeke. He proceeded to look for a restaurant or bar that could serve him a Manhattan while he waited for Abby. He had acquired a taste for Manhattans, but when he spotted a Tex-Mex, he changed his mind and opted for a margarita. He went up to the bar and ordered a lime margarita on the rocks, top shelf, patron, no salt with a maraschino cherry. When the bartender brought out the margarita, Zeke tried to pick out the maraschino cherry, but someone from behind beat him to the punch. He turned around to find Abby standing there with his maraschino cherry.

“What are you doing here so early?”

“I could ask you the same thing,” said Abby.

“I had to beat all the three forty-five road closings along Rock Creek Parkway,” said Zeke. “So, I came early.”

“Me too,” said Abby. “I thought I’d stop in here for a happy hour drink.”

"Well, since we're here. How about an appetizer before skating?"

"Sounds good to me," said Abby.

Zeke motioned to a waiter to seat them. While they waited for a table, Zeke ordered Abby a margarita and another maraschino cherry for himself.

After they got a table, the waiter brought some nachos. They ordered an appetizer of cheese filled jalapeños.

"So, did you enjoy Williamsburg?" asked Zeke.

"It was OK," said Abby.

"Just OK?"

"Well, I enjoyed being with you much more," said Abby. They sat gazing into each other's eyes until the margarita and jalapeños arrived. Abby picked up one of the jalapeños and placed it gently on Zeke's lips. Zeke took a bite. Then, he did the same with Abby. They took an occasional sip of their margaritas. This continued until they ate two of the four jalapeños. Then, Zeke said, "Let's do some skating."

"OK," said Abby. "But, I'm not very good. I'll need some help."

"No problem," said Zeke.

They rented some skates and went out on the ice. Zeke stood facing Abby, skating backward while Abby tried to keep her balance and get some forward motion. He held her in his arms at first and then moved his arms away holding her hands as she balanced. He looked into her beautiful light blue eyes.

"Abby, I just learned some very disturbing news. Actually, I haven't fully processed this myself yet."

"What is it?"

"I don't know how to say this." said Zeke.

"Just say it," said Abby.

"I just found out that Agent Johnson was an accomplice in the assassination attempt."

"What?" asked Abby "You must be mistaken. There's no way."

"It's true. He admitted to it. Told me himself."

"I can't believe it," said Abby.

"Neither can I. If I hadn't heard it with my own ears, I still wouldn't believe it. I think you can skate by yourself now," said Zeke as he let go of her hands. He wasn't ready to ask her any questions.

The End

Sneak Preview

In Book 1 of *Soul Reader*, Zeke Jackson finally believes that he has received a divine gift which he has already used to foil an assassination attempt on the president and vice president. But God has bigger plans for this flawed hero. Join him in Book 2, as this touch-enabled, real-time interactive, spirit-powered psychometric wades further into the swamp and uses his divine gift for such a time as this. And, see if the relationship with Abby pans out.

About the Author

Dante F. Lupinetti has lived in the greater Washington DC area for fifty years. Married with five grown children and nine grandchildren, Dante retired from a software engineering career after spending forty-five years commuting around the DMV (DC, Maryland, Virginia) as he worked for various defense contractors and commercial companies. Dante has been an elder in his church and he and his wife, Sue, lead a small group Bible study.

Check out my Facebook Page.
(https://www.facebook.com/soulreader/?view_public_for=105120427965920)

Hey! Sly McDonald here, Zeke's nefarious co-worker. Just a snippet of your time. This Dante guy, he worked tirelessly to bring Soul Reader to life, and he's not done yet. He's got some really, good stuff coming in the Soul Reader Series that'll keep you engaged, intrigued and thrilled. So, the best thing that you can do to help him keep going is to PLEASE LEAVE A REVIEW ON AMAZON. Oh, and sign up to his newsletter.

Bonus Content

How would you like to be a character in my next book in the Soul Reader Series? I will randomly select one of my fans who sign up for my newsletter.

Click https://www.subscribepage.com/soulreadersignup for a chance to be a character in my next book and to get exclusive access to the Soul Reader newsletter.

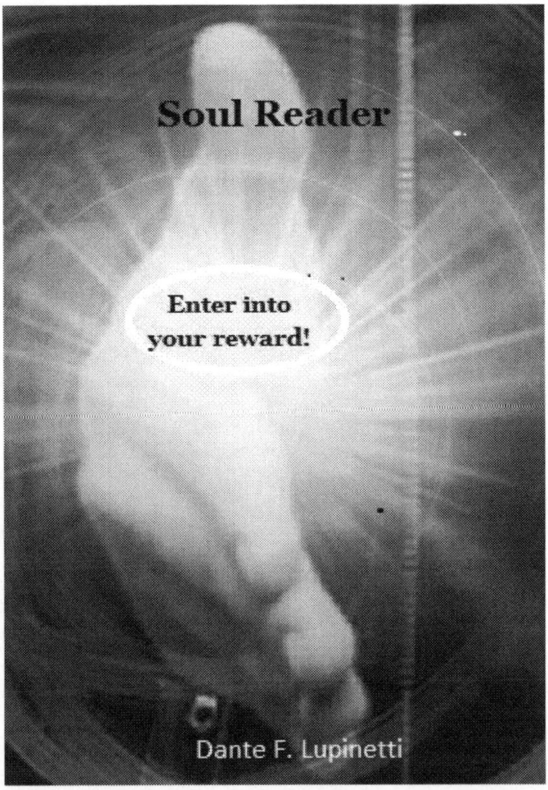

Made in the USA
Middletown, DE
13 March 2023

26580831R00163